HAWAI'I SPOOKY TALES 3

MORE TRUE LOCAL SPINE-TINGLERS

COLLECTED BY
RICK CARROLL

BESS PRESS

3565 Harding Ave, Honolulu, Hawai'i 96816
(808) 734-7159 fax (808) 732-3627 www.besspress.com

For my mother, Darralene M. Carroll,
who, at the turn of the century, turns 80.

Design: Carol Colbath
Moon logo from a design by Kevin Hand
Gourd helmet: Courtesy Tricia Allen

Library of Congress Cataloging-in-Publication Data

Carroll, Rick
    Hawaii's best spooky tales 3 : more true local
spine-tinglers / collected by Rick Carroll.
        p.   cm.
    Includes illustrations.
    ISBN 1-57306-100-X
    1. Ghost stories, American – Hawaii.
2. Tales – Hawaii. 3. Legends – Hawaii.
I. Title.
GR580.H3.C371 1999   398.25-dc20

Printed in the United States of America

ISBN 1-57306-100-X

Acknowledgments

To the thousands of people in Hawai'i and beyond who buy these small, important books and read the wonderful stories . . .

To each contributing author who helps keep alive Hawai'i's great storytelling tradition . . .

To The Bess Press, especially Benjamin Bess, Revé Shapard, Carol Colbath, Jeela Ongley, and Lori Bodine, who continue to support Hawai'i's cultural renaissance with words and pictures and deeds . . .

To all my friends in Hawai'i's public and school libraries who keep young readers reading and my books on the shelf . . .

To those who've told me stories yet to see print (please, be patient, the end is not in sight) . . .

To all of you, I can only say: Thank you. Without you, this book (and the three that preceded it) would only be stories I heard waiting to be shared.

Now, they are your stories, too.

They always were.

Aloha and mahalo

Rick Carroll

Contents

Introduction vii

Haunted Places 1

Spirits in the Living Room • *Robert S. Tripp* 3

The Elevator Man • *Reggie K. Bello* 8

Giving the Ghost a Lift • *Robert W. Bone* 12

Gaylord • *Nicole Howe* 17

Signs 21

No One Home • *Marcie Carroll* 23

Whispering Tree • *Sonny Kaukini Bradley* 28

Matching Numbers • *Jachin Hsu* 31

Ka Hōʻailona • *Charles Kauluwehi Maxwell, Sr.* 36

Sounds, Tastes, and Smells 41

A Piano for Liliʻu • *Van Love* 43

The Spirit of the Shade Tree • *Simon Nasario* 48

Disappeared • *Carolyn Sugiyama Classen* 51

Something Came Between Them • *Brian & Gigi Valley* . 55

The Vibes of Elvis • *John Flinn* 59

Night Visitors 65

Midnight Haircut in Kalihi • *Maria de Leon* 67

The Ghost in the Wall • *Steve Heller* 70

Impressions of Lānaʻi • *Ann Donohue* 77

Dream or Ghost at Kaunolū? • *Joana McIntyre Varawa* . 81

A Ghostly Tribe • *Michael Hocker* 84

The Graveyard Shift at ʻEwa • *Simon Nasario* 86

Nature and Spirits *89*

   Missing Man • *Steve Heller* 91

   Listen to the Wind • *Hannah J. Bernard* 98

   On the Wettest Spot in the World • *Robert Wenkam* . . 102

Saying Aloha *107*

   A *Pilialoha* with Pele • *Michael Sturrock* 109

   Searching for Aiko • *Kaui Philpotts* 112

   Sherry Lee • *Richard S. Fukushima* 116

   The Last *Aloha* • *Suzan Gray Bianco* 120

   August Butterflies • *Claire Ikehara, Nyla Fujii-Babb,*
                          Mary Ann Collignon 123

Royal Encounters • *Rick Carroll* *129*

   Lament for a Dead Princess 132

   Queen Emma Returns to the Summer Palace 133

   The Place Where Kalākaua Died 134

Personal Encounters • *Rick Carroll* *137*

   Forbidden Village 139

   On the Beach 143

   When *Kūpuna* Fly 145

   Old Bones 146

   The Halloween Waiter 148

About Rick Carroll

Author and travel writer Rick Carroll is a former daily journalist for the *San Francisco Chronicle*. He later covered Hawai'i and the Pacific for United Press International with a Nikon and a notebook.

His self-illustrated articles on Rapa Nui (Easter Island) and Huahine (Society Islands), have won the Lowell Thomas Award of the Society of American Travel Writers and the Gold Award of the Pacific Asia Travel Association. His reports from Manila and the Southern Philippines during the Marcos era won a national Headliner's Award.

Hawai'i's Best Spooky Tales 3 is Carroll's fourth collection of true accounts of inexplicable encounters in the Islands. He has shared these stories with audiences throughout the islands through personal appearances at schools, libraries, bookstores, and conferences. He was a 1997 Visiting Artist on Lāna'i and performed at the Bankoh Talk Story Festival on O'ahu.

He is also the author of six guidebooks, including *Great Outdoor Adventures of Hawaii*, and is co-editor of *Travelers' Tales Hawaii*, an anthology of personal discoveries in the Hawaiian Islands (O'Reilly & Associates, San Francisco).

Carroll lives in Hawai'i and Friday Harbor, Washington.

Introduction

'A'ole 'oe, no kēia hālau, no laila 'a'ole no 'oe i 'iki i ko'u po'opo'o.

You are not of my house; therefore, you do not know the secret of its closets.

—Hawaiian proverb

Dozens of ethnic groups are represented in Hawai'i, and so too, it appears, are their ghosts. Or whatever haunts them. No greater possibility of supernatural encounters exists on other islands of the Pacific, or for that matter anywhere else. Hawai'i is a cosmopolitan center of spiritual delight. Or horror, depending on your point of view.

This mysterious fact of island life is abundantly clear in *Hawai'i's Best Spooky Tales 3*, a collection of amazing stories that could surface only here. In this collection, you will discover all new, original, true stories from each island, including, for the first time, stories from the once "forbidden" Island of Ni'ihau.

If you are looking for "don't take pork over the Pali" stories, look elsewhere. Here, we present the real, scary stuff that can and does happen to anyone, especially those who scoff at old Hawaiian ways.

To pass my test, each story must deliver that delicious shiver everyone in the Islands calls "chicken skin." Let met tell you, this book delivers.

The varied stories in the voices of *kama'āina*, Native Hawaiians, and frequent travelers amount to eyewitness testimony that there's a lot more going on in Hawai'i after dark—sometimes in broad daylight—than anyone ever imagined.

Hawai'i's Best Spooky Tales 3 is wider in scope and deeper in mystery than its predecessors. It is full of new cultural revelations by Native Hawaiians. It includes oral histories, memoirs, and personal accounts of episodes certain to raise the hair on the back of your neck and shiver your bones. *Hawai'i's Best Spooky Tales 3* may be the best of all.

This collection features five outstanding new stories by Native Hawaiians: hula teacher Van Love; *kahu* and storyteller Charles

Kauluwehi ("Uncle Charlie") Maxwell, Sr.; master canoebuilder Sonny Kaukini Bradley; well-known storyteller Nyla Fujii-Babb; and author and newspaper columnist Kaui Philpotts.

We also present cultural and heritage stories from Japanese-American, Chinese-American, and Filipino-American authors. Oh, sure, you say, people of Polynesian and Asian ancestry all believe in that stuff. In response, may I direct your attention to equally chilling stories by former skeptics, some "local," some not: an Asia-Pacific airline captain, a Seattle veterinarian, a globe-trotting travel writer and photojournalist, a Kansas university professor now writing a novel about Lāna'i, and three Hawai'i librarians, whose stories will make you look twice at the next butterfly you see.

All these first-person, eyewitness accounts of strange encounters add up to a growing body of evidence that proves that what is extraordinary elsewhere is fairly common in the Islands. In Hawai'i we are surrounded by the inexplicable. It is the nature of the place and the people.

Stranger Beware

A caveat for visitors: If you're going to Hawai'i, watch your step. I don't mean O'ahu's big North Shore waves or steep cliffs called *pali*, or even the red-hot lava spilling out of Kīlauea Volcano. I'm not concerned, either, with commonsense guidebook warnings about not leaving your wallet on your beach mat.

I'm talking about serious things here—stuff nobody can explain, like a seaweed found only in a tidepool in Hāna that contains one of the deadliest biotoxins on earth. Or a lava tube that exudes the breath of Madame Pele. Surreal stuff like night marchers that tramp through your house. Hula dancers who develop auras at Ahu o Laka. *Pōhaku* (rocks) that cause intense headaches until they are replaced. Old royal graves that expose blank when photographed.

Here in *Hawai'i's Best Spooky Tales 3* you will meet the people who actually encountered or experienced things they can't explain. You may even wish to attempt to duplicate their experiences by visiting any of the sacred and powerful places identified in their stories. Or you may decide to check out The Guide to Spooky Places, which appeared in *Hawai'i's Best Spooky Tales* and *Hawai'i's Best Spooky Tales 2*. Either way, you'll discover a Hawai'i never found in guidebooks or travel magazines.

A Brief Preview

Some stories are so scary you probably shouldn't read them alone. I am thinking of "The Graveyard Shift in 'Ewa," by Simon Nasario, who saw eerie glowing lights rise out of graves one night, and "Midnight Haircut in Kalihi," by Maria De Leon, who even today gets chicken skin remembering what happened to her while she slept safely at home.

Tension is palpable in "Impressions of Lāna'i," by Anne Donohue, whose "pressing affair" at The Lodge at Kō'ele prompts her to sleep there now only with a night light.

Carolyn Sugiyama Classen, who regularly visits her father's grave on O'ahu and brings his favorite snack, discovers something very weird in "Disappeared."

Brian Valley sets out in search of sandalwood seeds on the Island of Lāna'i with a pal and discovers "Something Came Between Them."

Reggie Bello meets "The Elevator Man" on his first night on the night shift at a Big Island resort that stands on a sacred footpath of *ali'i.*

Jachin Hsu runs a footrace over O'ahu's H-3 freeway and finds signs that it was meant to be in "Matching Numbers."

On her second attempt to visit the forbidden island of Ni'ihau, Marcie Carroll encounters some eerie creatures but otherwise finds "No One Home."

Voices of the People

What always amazes me is the wide range of stories told by so many different people in so many different voices. Professional writers, unpublished contributors, frequent visitors, long-time residents— each has a spooky story to tell.

Joana McIntyre Varawa of Lāna'i, author of three books, including *The Delicate Art of Whale Watching,* fell asleep on a sunny afternoon visit to King Kamehameha's fish retreat on Lāna'i and awoke to wonder if what she saw was a "Dream or Ghost at Kaunolū?"

O'ahu-based travel writer Robert W. Bone tries to explain what happened to him when he rode an elevator in downtown Honolulu with his son, David, in "Giving The Ghost a Lift."

Kaua'i resident Richard S. Fukushima describes a moving encounter with the spirit of his niece in "Sherry Lee."

And John Flinn, travel editor of the *San Francisco Examiner,* makes a pilgrimage to a half-century-old ketchup stain on a derelict Kaua'i hotel's carpet to soak up The "Vibes of Elvis."

The collection includes stories from two young, budding authors: Nicole Howe, a La Pietra student, discovers her school is haunted in a chilling story about her spirit friend, "Gaylord." Michael Hocker, of McAllen, Texas, explains what he saw on an overnight stay in a Waikīkī hotel in "A Ghostly Tribe."

Nature of the Place

With lava tubes, cloud forests, and spinner dolphins, Hawai'i's own surreal nature is a dominant, sometimes unseen, force in several stories, including

• "Listen to the Wind," by Hawai'i adventurer Hannah J. Bernard, whose experience on Moloka'i is at once mystical and foreboding.

• "On the Wettest Spot in the World," by award-winning Hawai'i photographer and author Robert Wenkam, who gets all wet while camping on Kaua'i's Mount Wai'ale'ale.

• "The Last Aloha," by Suzan Gray Bianco, a story that will shiver any ocean swimmer who's ever encountered a moving object in the water larger than he or she is.

• Michael Sturrock's recollection of the day he discovered a sign on the front page of the *Honolulu Star-Bulletin* in a memoir entitled "A *Pilialoha* with Pele."

In "Royal Encounters," you will discover, as I did, that strange things still occur in and around the last earthly haunts of Hawai'i's kings and queens.

And, finally, I share with you my own personal encounters in these islands, including a visit to Hawai'i's last "Forbidden Village."

The great Russian poet and novelist (and butterfly collector) Vladimir Nabokov once said that the mark of all good writing and good reading is a chill up and down your spine. Judging by the chills up and down my spine just holding *Hawai'i's Best Spooky Tales 3*, I know you're in for another good read.

As always, of course, the faint-of-heart are advised never to read this book alone, after dark.

Or else.

Rick Carroll
Honolulu, Hawai'i

Haunted Places

Spirits in the Living Room

The Elevator Man

Giving the Ghost a Lift

Gaylord

On Kaua'i you still see old plantation houses, some of them restored and even clustered into new villages in Waimea on Kaua'i, 'Ewa on O'ahu, and Lāna'i City on Lāna'i. The houses are simple yet compelling because of their honest architecture. I have always wanted to live in one like my frend Robert Tripp's; he bought an old plantation home in the village of Kekaha on Kaua'i and settled down to enjoy the quiet life, never expecting to find . . .

Spirits in the Living Room

When I had the chance to buy the tiny, 400-square-foot plantation house I had been renting, it was necessary to state its age for the appraiser and insurance company. The lady from whom I was buying it was strangely evasive. It was agreed that "pre–World War II" would satisfy the requirements, but we all knew it was older by far.

The town of Kekaha had been culturally and physically dominated by the sugar mill since it was built in 1878. By 1980, when I moved there, changes had of course taken place, but plantation attitudes still prevailed and haoles made up only a small part of the population. It was what I was looking for. I enjoyed the cultural differences, and Kekaha provided a slow-paced haven from my schedule as an airline pilot on international routes. Of course, the year-round warm water and good surf was an added attraction for an old surf dog like me.

I made very few changes to the house when I moved in. The simplicity of the four small rooms—kitchen, living room, bedroom, bathroom—appealed to me. The furnishings, including the table, chairs, desk, dresser, and bed, were already there or purchased locally at moving or garage sales. Though most weren't as old as the house, they complemented its old-time style and feel.

Over the years, I have found that it is important for me to live in a place surrounded by physical beauty and tranquillity. Kaua'i certainly fills that need. Most of my flights were to the centers of commerce in the Orient—Tokyo, Seoul, Taipei, Bangkok. When the airline shut down the Honolulu base, I commuted back to Los Angeles twice a month rather than move. This made my time on Kaua'i even more precious.

Almost by osmosis I began to pick up the stories and legends of the islands. Those concerning Pele and the *menehune* I found particularly compelling. To this day I feel that the tales of the *menehune* have a core of truth that almost always lies behind the ethnic mythic lore of any cohesive society.

I knew of the night marchers and learned the importance of an *'aumakua* to each family for guidance and protection. I could see the influence of these legends in the customs of the local people around me, but I did not see them intruding directly into my life. Then one night all that changed.

My partner and I were finishing a fairly typical day for us—a late-afternoon swim, and surf extending into the sunset. We made it a point to experience the curtain closing on each day. This time of transition was the perfect point to allow quiet reflection and appreciation of the beauty that surrounded us.

Afterward we watched the first stars come out as we used our outdoor shower to wash the salt from our bodies. During our simple wok dinner we decided it was time to clean the bedroom. To do so, we moved the two wooden chairs from the bedroom to join those of the living room. Unconsciously, we left them all in a pattern of a rough circle.

Back in the bedroom we resumed our chores. At some point I turned to go back through the door to the living room to retrieve a chair. As I looked into the room I came to a shocked standstill. It was as though the air in the room had become liquid. It appeared as the ocean does when you are beneath the surface and a wave passes overhead. There seemed to be a shimmering presence in each chair. Intangible but undeniable was their presence. I felt as though I had intruded upon a meeting place of some secret society. The hairs raised on the back of my neck and I could feel the icy flash of adrenaline course through my body.

I backed up from the doorway and at the same moment felt the light touch of my partner's body. The thought that I might somehow be hallucinating this was eliminated when she whispered, "Do you feel that? Can you sense them?"

I nodded my head in agreement, feeling validated— one definition of reality is anything on which two people can agree.

We both backed up slowly into the bedroom, and then quietly exited outside. I could feel her hand trembling in mine, or was it mine in hers? What was happening here?

We both decided that somehow the arrangement of chairs we had made precipitated the conditions that allowed the event to happen. Neither of us felt threatened in any way but we also did not want to interfere with whatever was going on. We walked around the yard for a while and then returned to the house that seemed normal except for a lingering sense of excitement and apprehension in our minds. With some hesitation we took the chairs back into the bedroom and after some intense discussion went to bed.

This occurrence was never repeated, even though we tried rearranging the chairs later in the same formation. So what really happened? Don't ask me. I'm not an expert on the occult. I just fly airplanes. I'm not even sure I should be writing this.

Has it changed me? Yes, in some ways. I am much more likely to listen intently to people's stories of weird events or extraterrestrial contacts. Who is to say what lies underneath the surface of each day's ordinary events.

Though it isn't really an explanation, an amplification of this experience occurred when we were discussing the eradication of the old town of Mana on the AMFAC plantation with a local Hawaiian lady. Plantation houses occupied for generations were moved from there to the Waimea Plantation Resort, where they were reconditioned as units for tourists.

The effect is quite pleasant, giving the ambiance of being in an old plantation town. However, there apparently are stories coming from the maids and some of the guests of strange appearances and events.

Our friend laughed and said, "What do they expect? They provide a new home and familiar surroundings for the spirits of those who lived there."

Robert S. Tripp is a retired airline pilot who flew DC-10s on international routes to Asia and the Pacific for thirty years. A flight test pilot for the Federal Aviation Agency, he is a member of the Society of Experimental Test Pilots. For the past eighteen years he has lived in a small plantation town on an outer island of the Hawaiian chain. His articles on aviation and sports have appeared in *Airways, Flying, Ocean Sports, Discover Africa, Road and Track, Invention and Technology* and *Science Digest*. His first novel, "Last Clear Chance," about a pilot who survives a disastrous crash on takeoff from Hong Kong's airport, is now making the rounds of publishers.

On the Big Island of Hawai'i's Kohala Coast, new resorts stand in lava fields along ancient and often sacred footpaths of *ali'i*—as a young hotel employee discovers when he encounters . . .

The Elevator Man

In the summer of 1992, I was a housekeeper at one of the resorts along the Kohala Coast of the Big Island. I was only seventeen years old and had been working at the hotel for six months when this incident occurred.

Toward the end of the day, my manager asked me if I wanted to stay and work the night shift to help cover for a sick call. Even though I had never worked at night before, I agreed to stay and work a double shift. I was assigned to one of the towers in the hotel that night, and all I had to do was tend to the housekeepers.

The first two hours went smoothly. The sun had set, and now I was seeing the hotel in a way I'd never seen it before—darker, quieter, with different workers. I was on the service landing of the fourth floor, and I needed to go up to the seventh floor to pick up dirty linen from one of the housekeepers.

I pushed the "up" button on the elevator panel and waited for the one working elevator. There are two service elevators in the tower, but the one on the right (as you face the elevators) broke during the morning shift and had not been running all day.

To my surprise, the elevator on the right opened and out walked a tall, dark, Hawaiian-looking man, wearing nothing but a dark red *malo*. I didn't think much of it, since the hotel had so many workers in different uniforms.

He acknowledged my presence with a simple nod. I walked into the elevator and pushed the seventh floor button. As the doors, closed I could see that Hawaiian guy still on the service landing looking at me.

The elevator went up to the seventh floor, but the doors did not open. Instead, the "SL" button lit up, and I started going down. (SL stands for "service level," which was the hotel's underground tunnel system.) It stopped at the service level, but again the doors did not open. Instead, the seventh floor button lit up again, and I was on my way back up.

The elevator kept going up and down without stopping. I started to panic. I pounded on the doors and yelled for help! I started to feel nauseous, because it felt like the elevator was going faster and faster. I then realized that the elevator had an emergency telephone located right under the button panel. When I picked up the telephone, it automatically dialed the Security Department. A security officer answered, and I told her that I was stuck in the elevator. She told me to hang on until an engineer got to the tower.

I stayed on the telephone with the officer until the elevator finally stopped on the fourth floor—where I had originally gotten on. I thanked the officer and hung up the phone. The doors opened, and to my amazement, that Hawaiian guy was still there! I walked out, and he started moving toward the elevator. I didn't even think about telling him that the elevator was acting weird. I was just so happy to be out. As he passed me, he let out a little laugh under his breath. He walked into the elevator, and the doors closed behind him.

I noticed that there was no sound coming from the elevator. It didn't sound like it was moving. Moments later, the other elevator opened (the one on the left), and out walked an engineer. He asked me if I was the person who was stuck in the elevator.

"Yes," I said, "but it was the other elevator."

He looked at me really weird and said, "What? That elevator was shut down all day for repairs. It's still not running!"

With his words, the image of the Hawaiian man and all the stories I'd ever heard about Hawai'i's haunted hotels ran through my mind. Did I just have a supernatural encounter?

Reggie K. Bello, currently a hotel assistant manager at the Hilton Waikoloa Village, was born and raised in North Kohala on the Big Island. He is a graduate of Kohala High School and Hawai'i Community College, and lives in Kamuela.

You step into the elevator. Others enter, forcing you back, crowding you elbow to elbow with strangers. You stand quietly, staring at the back of the neck of the person in front of you. You wait for the elevator to go. That moment can seem like an eternity. Then the elevator door closes and up or down you go in silence, barely breathing until you arrive safely at your floor. Sometimes, though, the elevator stops at certain floors and nobody gets on or off. Is it only a mechanical glitch or are you . . . .

Giving the Ghost a Lift

Among the devices in the modern world that spook some folks are elevators.

It's not simply the claustrophobic effect of occupying a relatively confined space alone or with a group of strangers.

To those affected, to step into an elevator is to put themselves at the mercy of an unnatural environment in an unknown dimension—a sense of being placed in some sort of purgatory, where there is no ground, no sky, no sense of time of day, since neither daylight nor the darkness of the real world can be perceived.

"I mean, where ARE you really?" I was once asked by Mary Alice, a colleague at *Popular Photography* in New York, who had spent an unscheduled hour motionless between some floor and another in a nonfunctioning elevator.

Like many, I have been trapped in an elevator a few times in my life with little ill effect. Once, in Rio de Janeiro, I forgot that electricity was being rationed on a rotating basis in different parts of the city. When I went to visit a woman at her apartment one evening, I forgot to ask her what time the *falta* was scheduled to occur in her neighborhood. I simply had to sit on the floor in the dark and wait it out.

But to some people, elevators are more sinister.

Once in Puerto Rico, I was with several reporters traveling together in a single car over country roads long past midnight to check out a reported sighting of the Virgin Mary by some residents of a small village far into the interior of the island.

To keep ourselves entertained on this somewhat metaphysical trip, we told ghost stories. One particularly spooky one was related by Paul, whose aunt once had a terrifying experience. She was about to enter an elevator in a Chicago skyscraper when she noted with some alarm that the operator of the device was a skeleton.

Paul said his aunt was startled enough to decide to step back, whereupon the skeleton shrugged its clavicles and closed the door. The car suddenly plunged to the basement, killing all aboard.

Well, perhaps not all, I observed, since the skinny operator would seem to have been dead already. Paul was not amused, however. After all it was his close relative who had narrowly escaped death.

Another truism, subscribed to by many who occasionally turn their attention to the supernatural world, is that for some unknown reason, children are more sensitive to influences from beyond the grave.

Who hasn't heard of poltergeists who center their noisy and sometimes damaging habits on a child? Adults would never have seen the Jabberwocky, would they? Centuries ago, children so possessed were sometimes put to death by terrified populations.

One day in Honolulu these two volatile elements came together, the sensitive child, and the purgatorial elevator.

I think it was in that office structure at 1000 Bishop Street where my son, David, then about ten, and I entered the elevator, perhaps on our way to visit Jeff

Portnoy, an attorney who was handling a lawsuit I was bringing against my publisher.

David was equipped with a vivid imagination, and I held his hyperactive hand to make sure he did not dash off on the wrong floor. One or two of the small clutch of fellow travelers in the vertical dimension lowered their eyes from the set of numbers for a moment to smile at my handsome little boy.

Midway in our journey, the elevator stopped at a floor that had been chosen by none of us. The doors opened.

David stepped back. We all waited. The doors closed again, with no apparent change in the number of passengers. David spoke up in an even voice:

"Dad, a ghost got on there, you know."

If there was any conversation in the car, it ceased immediately.

"How did you know it was a ghost?" I asked, looking around at faces whose smiles had disappeared. All were listening intently.

"'Cause I could see right through him!" David replied.

There was a gasp or two of nervous, hollow laughter from those surrounding us.

One man quickly reached forward and pushed a new button for the very next floor. He apparently decided to leave immediately on an unscheduled stop. The rest of us decided to take our chances, and the door closed once more.

"Don't worry, Dad. It's all right," said David. "The ghost got off with him!"

Kailua resident Robert W. Bone is the author of four travel guidebooks and numerous travel articles that appear frequently in newspapers and magazines on the mainland.

He maintains a web site at http://members.aol.com/robertbone.

Any new student is bound to
encounter rites of passage.
Nicole Howe never suspected
she would be one of
the lucky La Pietra
students to discover what
school spirit really means in
this haunting story about . . .

Gaylord

Any student entering a new school is bound to encounter rites of passage, but meeting Gaylord was an experience I never expected.

As a first-year student at La Pietra, a small all-girls school on O'ahu, I was spoon-fed all sorts of pertinent information about the school:

It is the former residence of Walter and Louise Dillingham, who were descendants of Benjamin Dillingham, a man who built his empire through sugarcane and the first railroad in Hawai'i. The house was constructed in the 1920s and is not the typical Diamond Head house.

The original structure was modeled after the Dillingham's house in Tuscany, Italy, also named La Pietra. With a distinct Mediterranean look, the campus is a pink-stucco masterpiece, with clay shingles, a U-shaped quad, and abundant sculptures.

Our campus also features beautiful white doves, a courtyard fountain filled with water lilies, and—a ghost? Gaylord is the one piece of history that will never be included in the school's brochure.

My introduction to Gaylord Dillingham occurred on what had been a normal morning. It was a few days before Halloween (no lie!), we were all in a spooky spirit, and I had arrived early on campus while dawn was still lingering.

I was on the second floor of the main building, looking

down into the courtyard, and I noticed the lights in the kitchen were flickering. When I pointed it out to my friend Natalie, who was standing beside me, she remarked that it was "just Gaylord."

I hadn't heard of anyone named Gaylord and might have let her remark pass, but her cryptic manner piqued my interest and I pestered her until she cracked and spilled the story, which was not at all what I expected.

You see, Gaylord is the school's resident ghost. Gaylord was the youngest of the Dillingham children, she explained, and he befell a strange fate.

On campus, the accepted story is that, as a small child, Gaylord was inadvertently locked in the basement (which is now our bookstore) and starved to death. Some people also tell that Gaylord is buried out by the back pond.

Hearing this, I was terrified. Had I actually witnessed a ghost trying to communicate? Or was it just the supervisor messing with the lights? It couldn't have been my imagination, since Natalie had also noticed this event.

I talked to other people who had heard stories about dark shadows and voices. The more I found out about Gaylord, the more I came to believe that the flickering lights weren't an isolated incident.

One story I heard was that a class of girls had run screaming out of a classroom in the middle of our annual Christmas program, claiming they had heard noises. The room they had run out of was once the master bedroom, where Gaylord's parents slept. And the adjoining room, now our French classroom, was once Gaylord's bedroom. When I heard about that, I didn't want to set foot in that room, but many of my friends thought I was just trying to avoid French class.

As I learned more about our school's supernatural legend, I became convinced that a spirit of some kind haunted our school.

Three years after my chance meeting with Gaylord, I met him again. While on a field trip to Oʻahu Cemetery with my Hawaiian history class, I wound up at the Dillingham family plot. There, right under my feet, lay the grave of Gaylord Dillingham.

He had died in 1945, a fighter pilot shot down in the days just before the end of World War II. His body was never found, for his plane splashed down into the sea and was never recovered. The mystery of Gaylord had been solved for me.

When I returned to school that afternoon, thoughts of the little boy whom we all knew but knew nothing about invaded my brain. I had a great desire to shout my discovery at the top of my lungs, but preferred to let Gaylord remain mysterious, a person to blame for Halloween tricks and overnight fears, our school's macabre mascot.

Gaylord does haunt our school; he watches over us and once in a while makes himself known, whether it be flickering lights or dark shadows in a crowded room.

He is there, I know.

Nicole Howe is currently a junior attending La Pietra-Hawaiʻi School for Girls. She lives in Kailua with her parents and her younger brother. An avid fan of horror stories, she loves everything from cheesy movies to a great ghost story. Nicole hopes to one day be a professional journalist.

Signs

No One Home

Whispering Tree

Matching Numbers

Ka Hōʻailona

Skulls of goats and wild pigs on wobbly last legs, hungry tiger sharks in blue lagoons, little precious sea shells on gold sand beaches littered with trash—it all seemed very eerie to a first-time visitor. If you go to the "forbidden" island of Ni'ihau do not expect palm trees or even a lei greeting from this atypical Hawaiian island. Be prepared, instead, to find . . .

No One Home

Of all the Islands, the one that held the most fascination for me was Niʻihau, mysterious, off-limits, fabled home of pure Hawaiians and the tiny shells they plucked from their beaches to fashion into exquisite jewelry. It was the shells that started this.

My first trip to Hawaiʻi many years ago was to the North Shore of Kauaʻi, where precious strands of tiny white, brown, and pink Niʻihau shells were displayed in a small gallery in Hanalei, for untouchable prices.

I wanted to go to Niʻihau someday and gather my own shells. I was intrigued by the tales of a living museum of a village ruled by a *kamaʻāina* family and filled with people who spoke Hawaiian and kept the old ways, who weren't allowed to return if they ever dared leave (no longer so). And I was not a little piqued by the idea that in late–twentieth-century America, the place was closed to innocent, well-intentioned me.

Some years later when we moved to the Islands, I watched a hula *hālau* from Niʻihau perform at a festival, bringing the past to life with their old-fashioned style of song and dance and dress, white *muʻumuʻu* adorned with breathtaking shell lei. Neighbors told me stories of how sailors and windsurfers would crash-land on the private island, only to be politely sent packing before they had a chance to contaminate the cultural atmosphere with their modern ways.

Then I had an unexpected chance to view the island, if only from a plane. A new flightseeing tour was being launched, to fly over the channel from Kaua'i to its low-profiled neighbor and back. The first flight was just for travel agents, writers, and photographers, and I was invited. We boarded after a sumptuous brunch at the newly opened Princeville Hotel on a sparkling, perfect day. But no sooner were we airborne than brisk trades turned into a vicious gale, howling and tossing the little plane like a toy.

We made it only halfway down the Nā Pali Coast. Several passengers, including me, promptly threw up. Others hit their heads on the ceiling of the aircraft during violent air-pocket drops and rises. Turbulence sent cameras and notebooks flying. Fear was growing in the cabin, along with an undeniable sense of NONONONONO, until finally a photographer and former Vietnam helicopter pilot yelled to the pilot, "Hey! Turn this thing around!!" The young pilot, surprised by a passenger revolt, said, "Really? Okay, sure," and did a 180-degree turn.

Instantly, calm was restored. White-knuckled passengers stopped shaking, breathed deep, and enjoyed the flawless view of Nā Pali. I was so grateful that it was with just a little regret I realized I wouldn't get to see Ni'ihau today. The flightseeing venture was short-lived.

But I got another chance a year or two later when Ni'ihau was suddenly opened to tourism—well, in a way—by the advent of a medical helicopter that did double duty as a flightseeing chopper. I was one of the first to pay $250 for the privilege of seeing Ni'ihau for an hour or two—after all, it was for a good cause, helping pay for Islanders' medical emergency flights. We boarded in West

Kaua'i and flew over the channel, cruised Lehua Crater, and then landed, at last, on a barren beach. We descended over a small deepwater landing, where we could see a dozen black bullet shapes in the water. Sharks. Waiting for the next load of cattle, perhaps, or maybe for us.

A handful of us prowled the virgin strand, a beachcomber's dream, found glass fishing floats, and tasted our first freshly plucked *'opihi*. Ni'ihau shimmered in a relentless sun, in the throes of a bad drought. Oddly, the beach was littered with white bones and curly-horned sheep skulls. No sign of life was visible, and we were carefully kept far away from the village or its people. We boarded the chopper and flew to another vacant beach, the historic one where Capt. James Cook is said to have dropped anchor before his ships landed at Waimea and officially "discovered" Hawai'i.

I strode a little faster than the rest. I wandered around one headland and found a mountain of tangled plastic trash, woeful relic of the world beyond here. I rounded another and crouched to search for shells. Gradually, after a few minutes, I realized I was no longer alone in the pocket cove.

I looked up—and stopped breathing when I saw the silhouettes of several wild pigs, all staring down at me from the edge of the low cliff. I turned slowly to find that between me and my exit, close enough to touch, was a big black hog, with long tusks and rough pig hair and glittery eyes. My heart pounded, and I froze in place. We stood there for endless moments. He did not move, so ever so slowly, I sidled around him. I made it to the headland and raced a short way down the beach.

Nothing followed me, and my companions were still too distant. Then curiosity pulled me back. Ready to run the other way at any time, I snuck a look around the headland at the pig beach. The silhouetted pigs had vanished. The big black hog was still there. He had fallen over in his tracks and died, presumably a victim of the drought. Or maybe he was fatally afraid of me, or perhaps he had simply done his guardian duty and departed.

We left soon after—everyone thought I made up the pigs, since no one else saw them or walked that far. Thoughtfully, I fingered a few tiny jewel shells in my pocket as we flew off, clearing the desolate clifftop in a swirl of red dust. Goodbye, Ni'ihau, still *kapu*.

Marcie Carroll left her job as editor of politics, law and government at the *San Francisco Chronicle* in the early 1980s, bought a one-way ticket to Hawai'i, and studied Japanese language and history on a Gannett Fellowship at the University of Hawai'i's Asian Studies Center. She traveled widely in Asia and the Pacific and returned to Honolulu to edit *Discover Hawaii* magazine and write about people, destinations and the travel industry. She joined the Hawai'i Visitors Bureau as director of communicatons, created prize-winning publications and worked with writers and broadcasters from around the world in pursuit of Hawai'i stories. In the '90s, she began a freelance writing/editing career from her Lanikai Beach home. A graduate of Bucknell University, she earned a masters in journalism from Stanford University. A frequent contributor to *Successful Meetings* magazine, she is co-editor of *Travelers' Tales Hawaii* (O'Reilly & Associates, San Francisco). She lives in Hawaii and Friday Harbor, Washington.

When I met Sonny Bradley, one of the last Hawaiian *koa* wood canoe builders, in the early '80s, I really had only one question: How do you know which tree is the right one for a canoe? I could tell he felt uneasy revealing the secret of his arcane craft—Hawaiians are that way—but I really wanted to know. "It's a feeling I get from the tree," he said. I asked him to describe the feeling and he told this enchanting story about how a bird in the forest once led him to the . . .

Whispering Tree

High above the sea on the slopes of Mauna Kea and far off the dirt roads, we search and scour the forest for a suitable koa tree to make a canoe.

The koa forest has dwindled today. To find a canoe log from what was once an abundant forest is challenging.

As we trek on foot through the lush, damp forest, a feathered friend appears conspicuously to keep us company, sometimes darting through the trees ahead of us as if to know where we're going.

In the serenity of the forest, we come upon a tree with shimmering crescent leaves; the bird is perched upon it.

Although it is not a perfect or straight canoe log, it captivates my attention. Not having the luxury of yester-years, one must be realistic and look for the "potentials" of a log.

My eyes eagerly scan every inch up and down the tree, evaluating the condition, shape, and growth pattern of the tree. Defects can be repaired. A crook in the log can be skillfully appropriated to the rocker of the canoe.

The bird flutters to and fro, to and fro, as if dancing with the tree or telling me something. The mountain breeze kicks up and the tree whispers to me.

I get chicken skin. I am enthralled with this tree.

An electrifying feeling goes through my bones, all the way down to my toes, when I see a canoe encased within the tree.

It wants to be let out! Something inside me urges and insists that I get that canoe out of the log.

I know instinctively that this is "the right canoe log."

In that moment I realize the bird has disappeared.

Sonny Kaukini Bradley is Hawai'i's premier canoe builder. His BRADLEYracer canoes, now made of fiberglass on O'ahu, are the fastest boats in Pacific waters today, annually coming in first in the Moloka'i Hoe, the race across Kaiwi Channel between Moloka'i and O'ahu, one of the deepest, most dangerous channels in any ocean. Bradley, who has resumed carving and handcrafting Hawaiian *koa* canoes, lives on O'ahu's Windward side with his wife, Momi-e, and daughter, Marissa.

In the alphanumeric culture of California's Silicon Valley, folks play close attention to numbers because they really mean something. In Hawai'i, the H-3 means something else: it's the nation's most expensive freeway, and it violated a sacred valley and caused a *kahuna* to impose a curse. Was it just a coincidence that Jachin Hsu, a computer programmer, returned home from a footrace over the H-3 and discovered . . .

Matching Numbers

I have traveled to many parts of the world, and Hawai'i has been by far my favorite destination. I would use any excuse for a visit to Hawai'i. Therefore, I was quite pleased when I read in *Aloha* magazine about the Heihei O Hālawa 'Ekolu (H-3) race to be held in May of 1997. I thought it might be fun to run in the race and then head over to Maui for a nice ten-day vacation. I was able to convince my co-worker, David Pulvino, to join me in this one-time race, and we began to make preparations.

We arrived on O'ahu on Friday, May 9 (two days before the race) and immediately headed over to the race headquarters to pick up our race packets. Both of us opened our race packets and found that they included our race badges, which were to be worn on the day of the race. I took one look at my number (12564), thought for a minute or so, and said to my co-worker, "Dave, this number looks really familiar, I think it's the same as my employee number!" He replied, "No way, not in a million years!" Well, I thought nothing more of it and we went ahead and participated in the race on Sunday.

We stayed in Hawai'i for another week after the race. While out shopping I purchased the book *Chicken Skin*, by Rick Carroll. When I arrived back home in California I read the book and became very interested in the story about the H-3 freeway. I also checked my employee badge and was able to prove to Dave and other co-workers that my race number and employee number were exactly the same. At the time, I just assumed it was some sort of coincidence.

I, of course, liked telling this story to anyone who would listen, so I hung my race badge on the wall in my cubicle (I'm an Oracle database programmer). About four weeks after the race, I was talking with another co-worker, Diane Friday, in my cubicle and she happened to be looking at my employee badge, which was hanging around my neck. It was on backward, with my employee number and hire date showing. She was looking at my hire date and she exclaimed, "Wow, you've been here a long time, over ten years, since 5/11/87!" Just as she stated that I happened to be looking at my H-3 race badge and noticed the date of the race—May 11, 1997! It was the same day, exactly ten years later! It was one thing to have my race number and employee number match, but also to have the date of the race and my hire date match—I just could not believe it! At the realization of the matching numbers and dates, I understood what it means to experience "chicken skin"! It was just a weird feeling. I got goose bumps all over!

When I look back at all my past experiences with Hawai'i, I realize how very unlikely it was that I was even a participant in the race. In the fall of 1995, some of my friends were planning a trip to Hawai'i in February of 1996. I had never been to Hawai'i, and I actually never had any desire to go. My image of Hawai'i was a crowded place full of tourists, so I had no desire to ever go there. Therefore, I declined the invitation of my friends. They, however, continued to ask me to go with them and I continued to say "No, thanks."

About one week before my friends were to leave for

Hawai'i, I received another call from a friend (Richard Lodenquai) who had just completed a very big project for his company (Sun Microsystems). As a bonus for completing the project on time, his employer was awarding the entire project team an all-expenses-paid trip to Hawai'i! He told me the dates of the trip, and I realized they coincided with the trip of my other friends, whom Richard also knew. I told Richard that he should get together with this other group of friends and have lunch with them. I wished him well and we hung up. Well, about two hours later he called back and asked me if I wanted to have lunch with them in Hawai'i! As it turns out, he was able to bring a guest and he did not have one, so he invited me. In fact, that day was the very last day to add a guest, and the cutoff time was at noon and when he called me back it was already 4:30 p.m. However, pulling a few strings he was able to add me at the last minute.

We had a great time in Kaua'i and on the Big Island, one of the best vacations I've ever had. As a result of that trip, I came back home wanting to learn more about Hawai'i, its people, and its culture. I bought books and even some Hawaiian language tapes. I also chose to subscribe to *Aloha* magazine as a way for me to keep up to date on the things that were going on in Hawai'i. And it was in the magazine that I read about the H-3 freeway race!

I have often tried to determine the odds of having my numbers match, but I have concluded that it was basically impossible for my numbers and the dates to match! I had tried my best to avoid going to Hawai'i, yet a way was still provided for me to get there through no effort of my own. If I had never gone on that free trip I would never have even tried to visit Hawai'i, I would never have fallen in love with the Hawaiian Islands, I would never have come back home wanting to learn more about Hawai'i, I would never have subscribed to *Aloha* magazine, I would never have run in the H-3 Freeway race, and I would have never had my matching numbers!

I have continued to tell this story to whomever I run into; in fact, I carry my race badge and my employee badge with me wherever I go. When others hear this story, most get a tingle down their spine and they tell me to play numbers in the California Lottery! I believe that all these circumstances have a purpose and a reason for happening, yet I cannot help but wonder, why?

Ever since his first visit to the Hawaiian Islands, Jachin Hsu has been searching high and low for a job in Hawai'i, but so far his quest has been fruitless. His hope is to someday move to Hawai'i, but for now he can only look forward to his next trip to the islands.

When seven Hawaiians reburied the last of a thousand and more bones of their ancestors unearthed during groundbreaking for a new resort hotel at Honokahua, Maui, in 1991, they experienced a spiritual and inspiring encounter unlikely to occur again, as one member of the burial party explains in . . .

Ka Hō'ailona
(The Sign)

The modern-day name for the uninhabited island seen off the coast of Wailea, Maui, is Kaho'olawe, though our chants tell us that its ancient name was Kanaloa. Kanaloa was a primordial god from antiquities, and was the deity for the ocean, its animals, fresh water, salt water, and all the growth on Earth and in the sea. On the northwest side of Kaho'olawe is Ahupū Bay, whose west point is called Lae o Nā Koholā, or Cape of Whales.

The *koholā* (whale) was well known to the early Hawaiians. In the Kumulipo chant—the Hawaiian chant of creation—the Second Era speaks of the birth of the whale: "*Hānau ka palaoa noho i kai*"—born is the whale living in the ocean. And the *paukū*, or poetic passages, address the familiar scene in native Hawaiian culture of whales parading through the 'Alalākeiki Channel between Maui and Kaho'olawe.

This seasonal phenomenon reminds us constantly that from the time of our native Hawaiian ancestral migration, Kanaloa and his many ocean forms were continuously associated with the island Kanaloa.

The whale is the largest ocean form, and a majestic manifestation of Kanaloa. From the ivory of this creature, the highly prized *niho palaoa* was worn by the *ali'i* (chiefs) of high rank. The scarcity and beauty of the *niho lei palaoa* and its connection to Kanaloa brought *mana* (spiritual power) to the carver, to the pendant itself, and eventually to the wearer of the pendant.

The *aliʻi* who possessed the *kino lau*, or body form, of this great god would themselves acquire the characteristics, intelligence, and knowledge of the god. Therefore, it would be advantageous for any *aliʻi* to secure the ivory whale tooth of this Kanaloa body form.

The *koholā* is revered in modern-day Hawaiʻi not only by the thousands of whale watchers, but by the native Hawaiians, who still consider it as one of Kanaloa's magnificent creations.

In 1990, I was one of the fortunate ones who were touched by the *koholā*. Several of us were involved in relocating the Ritz-Carlton Hotel in Honokahua. Originally, the hotel was supposed to be built over ancient Hawaiian burial grounds. After strong objections from the Hawaiian community, it was relocated to its present site.

I was one of seven people chosen to rewrap the thousands of remains that had been dug up. The remains dated between A.D. 850 and the early 1800s. There were numerous *niho lei palaoa* (whale tooth necklaces), from one to six inches in length. This would indicate that royalty of all ages were interred with their symbols of nobility.

In 1991 a very spiritual incident occurred on the last night that we buried the last remains at Honokahua. At midnight, we were ready to start our burial rituals when we heard a loud slapping coming from Honokahua Bay.

As we looked over the hill into the bay we saw an outline of a whale lying on its side, rhythmically hitting the water with its pectoral fin. After about fifteen minutes it stopped, and we went back to the burial pit.

As we started our ceremonies, several owls flew overhead and screamed, then headed for the mountains. This was the Hōʻailona, the sign that our *kūpuna* were back reunited with their *iwi*, bones.

While the burials were taking place, a song came to me, which tells of the night's events. The name of the song is "Ka Hō'ailona" (the sign), recorded by the Pandanus Club in 1992, from the compact disc called "Te Tama."

In English it says:

> At midnight the conches blew as one
> Summoning the spirits back
> With the flames from the torches as a guide
> They came from the heavens above
>
> They came from Tahiti and Aoetealoa (New Zealand)
> To continue their eternal rest
> And again reunite with their bones
> In this land called Honokahua
>
> They did not know how to thank these men
> Who laid their bones to rest
> So they called upon the *koholā*
> Who slapped the waters of the bay
>
> In view was an owl, indeed it is a sign
> Their presence are here our great ancestors
> Inhaled was their fragrance, by the
> Beautiful blossoms, today's people
> In Honokahua, yes the adornment of Maui
>
> We will always remember
> The place of my birth
> Where the sign was given
> that our *kūpuna* (ancestors) are at rest.

Charles Kauluwehi (Uncle Charlie) Maxwell, Sr., was born on Maui about a mile from the Honokahua burials at Nāpili. A *kahu* and storyteller, Uncle Charlie also is a songwriter and creator of the song "Honokahua Nani E," which was recorded by the Pandanus Club in 1989 and won the Album of the Year at the 1990 Nā Hoku Hanohano. His story "Ka Hōʻailona" originally appeared in *Nā Poʻe Hawaiʻi*. Other stories by Uncle Charlie may be enjoyed on his web page: hookele.com.storyteller.

Sounds, Tastes, and Smells

A Piano for Lili'u

The Spirit of the Shade Tree

Disappeared

Something Came Between Them

The Vibes of Elvis

A gift to Hawai'i's last reigning monarch, the piano made in New York from Big Island *koa* wood was presented to Queen Lili'uokalani in 'Iolani Palace on her fifty-third birthday more than one hundred years ago. You can see the piano today in Honolulu's Washington Place, where Aunty Lei discovered that something wasn't right about . . .

A Piano for Lili'u

It was a beautiful morning! The sun was shining and my mother and aunt were looking forward to visiting Washington Place. They were to visit the home that my mom's great-great grandfather Isaac Hart built for John Dominis many years ago.

We are *'ohana* (family) to Lili'u, and it is always a joy to visit the beautiful home that the governor of Hawai'i now resides in.

Mom and Aunty Lei checked in at the front and were waiting for a guide to come and take them on a tour of Lili'u's home. They had gone into the portrait room, where life-sized portraits of King Kalākaua and Queen Lili'uokalani dominate the room. Mom was standing in front of Kalākaua, and Aunty Lei was looking at the portrait of Lili'u. They were both thinking about the king and queen and how it must have been when they were alive. It was as if they were communicating with them somehow through the ages.

Continuing into another portion of the house, they came to a group of children standing in front of a grand piano. Someone in the group asked if anyone could play, and since my aunt is an accomplished piano player, she volunteered. Aunty sat at Lili'u's piano and started to play, but the sounds coming out of the piano were very strange. My aunt looked puzzled and started again. The music was deep and low, with a heavy bass sound. Mom asked my aunt what was wrong and my aunt said, "I'm not sure. These heavy sounds are the only ones coming out. I feel a very strong masculine presence here." She started again, and again the sounds were deep and heavy.

Mom said, "I've never heard you play like this before, Lei. What's going on?"

Aunty Lei said, "I don't know. I can't figure it out! It's as though Lili'u is trying to tell me something. I keep feeling a heavy masculine energy. I wonder why?"

After one more attempt, my aunt gave up, saying that this was the first time she was unable to play a piano. (Aunty Lei started playing the piano at the age of seven and has been a mentor for students from time to time.) She stood up and they walked away and waited for their guide.

The docent soon came to take them on their tour of Washington Place. They couldn't shake their strange experience with the piano, but tried to enjoy the tour anyway. When the docent came to the piano, she told its story:

Lili'u had been given the piano on the evening of May 12, 1892. It was presented to her in the throne room of the palace. The presentation "was made by Messers, [sic] John Phillips, J. H. Soper, and J. F. Hackfeld, the committee appointed for that purpose."[1]

The piano was a gift for Lili'uokalani's fifty-third birthday, and it was intended to be "as Hawaiian as possible."[2] A huge *koa* tree from the island of Hawai'i was cut and shipped to the J. & C. Fischer piano company of New York.[3]

The interesting note here is that some of the group that presented the piano to Lili'u were instrumental in the overthrow of the Hawaiian monarchy in January, 1893.

John Harris Soper, who was born in Plymouth, England, came to Hawai'i in 1877. He began a career here, raising sugar, and was the manager of the Pioneer Mill in Lahaina, Maui. He was the head of the force that suppressed the Robert Wilcox rebellion of 1889. Soper was also asked to head the forces of the Provisional Government and it was under his command that the monarchy was overthrown. In January, 1894, he was commissioned as general in the National Guard, and he also suppressed the counterrevolution of 1895.[4]

Heinrich Hackfeld was born in Oldenburg, Germany, and came to Hawai'i around 1848. He developed a business of importing machinery and supplies for the sugar plantations and exported raw sugar.[5]

Many of the men who decided to have this beautiful piano made for the queen were the business elite or known to be sympathetic to them. It is interesting that they would have given Lili'u such a gift to gain her confidence when shortly thereafter they were plotting her overthrow.

After hearing this story on the history of Lili'u's piano, Aunty Lei turned to my mother and said, "That's it! That's why I felt the masculine energy. That's why I was feeling a sadness surrounding the piano. Lili'u doesn't like this piano. She does not want it in her home. Was this a gift of love? I know now that she was trying to tell me that she is not comfortable with this piano here."

Now everything became very clear. Hawaiians call this *puka mai*, "to make clear " or "to make known." Some of the men who gave Lili'u the piano were the ones who eventually overthrew her monarchy. Mom and Aunty Lei stood there looking at each other, wondering what to do.

That's where I come in. When they first told me this story, we knew that Lili'u's spirit was trying to get her message across. I know that she must trust my mother and my aunt very much. Maybe because we all are family. Maybe because Aunty Lei is very spiritual. Whatever her reason, I feel that she wants this story told.

I'm not sure how you feel about spirits, but I do believe they exist. I have had personal experiences that would be considered in the realm of the supernatural. Because things are unexplainable, does not mean they didn't happen. Because we can't see something, does not mean it doesn't exist.

When I spoke to Aunty Lei recently she said, "I know some people will not believe this. That's okay. Your mother was there to witness what happened, and I know that I do not want to ever play that piano again."

[1] "A Royal Piano," *Daily Pacific Commercial Advertiser*, p. 6.
[2] "A Royal Piano," p. 6.
[3] "Queen Lili'uokalani's Piano Will Be Sent to San Francisco to Be Shown at Diamond Jubilee," *The Honolulu Advertiser*, 14 June 1925, p. 8.
[4] Day, A. Grove, *History Makers of Hawaii*, Honolulu: Mutual Publishing, 1978.
[5] Day, *History Makers of Hawaii*.

Van Love is a Hawaiian Studies teacher and the granddaughter of a *kumu hula*. She started learning the hula shortly after she was born and today is a *kumu hula* herself.

Progress always involves change—sometimes in different realms. Trees come down, lots get cleared, buildings go up. In Hawai'i, the slightest change in the landscape can and often does trigger a mysterious, painful affliction, as Simon Nasario reveals in this true story from "small kid time" in 'Ewa about his uncle and . . .

The Spirit of the Shade Tree

Sometime back in 1932, my uncle wanted to build a carport in back of his house in 'Ewa, but there was a big tree in the way. So he decided to chop down part of the tree to make room for his carport.

A few weeks later he noticed a severe pain in his right arm and shoulder, so he went to the hospital to have the doctor check him out. The doctor said he couldn't find anything wrong, but he did give him something to rub on it and told him to use a hot pad. But this failed to give him any relief from the pain.

So he told an old-timer about his having such pain and how the doctor's remedy didn't seem to help. The old-timer said, "Moah bettah you see one *kahuna*. Maybe they can help you." So he took my uncle to an old *kahuna* lady over Kīpapa-side, that's near Honouliuli.

The old *kahuna* lady took one look at my uncle and said, "You go. You no believe. I no can help you."

But my uncle somehow managed to convince her that he really did believe in the old Hawaiian way, so she let him into her house.

"What kine *pilikia* you got?" she asked him.

So he told her.

She touched and *lomi lomi* his arm and shoulder awhile then asked him, straight out, "You chop down one tree behind your house?"

He told her that he had and asked her why she wanted to know.

She told him that there was an old Japanese man buried there many years before and he get "plenny *huhū* wit' you."

"This tree only shade he get," she told him. "Now you must make sacrifice to him, then he let go your arm and shoulder so you can feel okay."

"What kine sacrifice?" my uncle asked.

She told him to get some mochi (rice cake) and sake (rice wine). Build an altar of stone. No need be too high, near the base of the tree trunk. Place the mochi and sake on the altar along with a couple of white paper strips about three inches wide on which she had written some Japanese characters. Place the white paper on one rock and hold it down with another, then place the mochi and sake on top of the top rock. He was to do this for three weeks, then all would be okay.

By golly, after three weeks, my uncle said the pain went away. Us kids never went near that tree. When we went anywhere, my uncle got the car out of the carport before we got in.

Simon Nasario was born in 'Ewa, O'ahu, where he also attended grade school. A 1938 graduate of McKinley High School, he served with D Company, 298th Infantry, from November 1941 to November 1945. A former worker at 'Ewa Plantation, he now lives on the mainland. Nasario also contributed "The Graveyard Shift at 'Ewa," on page 86.

In Hawai'i people often hold picnics in graveyards; they bring food and drink and spread a blanket to spend the afternoon with dear, departed family members. Sometimes, like this devoted daughter, they bring their deceased relative a favorite food. She always brought her father's favorite dessert to his grave in a Big Island Buddhist cemetery. And each time it . . .

Disappeared

My beloved father, Dr. Francis Sueo Sugiyama, passed away on May 8, 1996. Dad was born in a small plantation village called Hala'ula in North Kohala on the Big Island. He grew up there, graduated from Kohala High School, attended the University of Hawai'i at Mānoa, and later got his dental degree from the University of Maryland. Because he loved Kohala, he returned to practice dentistry and orthodontics in Hāwī for thirty years.

We all remember his favorite dessert—sliced bananas topped with peanut butter. Dad would eat this several times a day. He belonged to the Kohala Jodo Mission in Kapa'au, where his parents, two brothers, and sister-in-law are at rest in the cemetery. So, of course, when he died, he was buried in this same small graveyard, next to its charming Buddhist mission in rural Kapa'au.

Something mysterious started occurring during the summer of 1998. Because Dad used to loved bananas so much, Mom began leaving a whole, unwrapped banana at his gravesite. One day Mom left a banana, as usual, on a small "table" on Dad's grave, which usually holds incense and other offerings in keeping with the Buddhist religion. Four hours later I stopped by to put flowers on Dad's grave, but nowhere did I see a banana. When I asked my Mom where she had put the banana, she insisted that she had left it as before, on the little table.

A few days later, my thirteen-year-old son, Stephan, and I left another banana at Dad's grave in the morning. When Mom visited in the early afternoon, the banana had once again disappeared.

Later that month, Stephan hid a banana under a fern that was growing on Dad's grave. This was a fairly large fern, and you couldn't see the banana when you walked by the grave. The next morning we anxiously returned, to find no trace of the banana. I felt chicken skin going down my back at that moment. Perhaps it was Dad's ghost eating the banana, and not a human thief as I had suspected, since a thief never would have seen that hidden banana.

This disappearance of the banana from Dad's gravesite went on all summer. Was it Dad's ghost returning from the dead to enjoy his favorite dessert? Japanese Americans believe in *obake*—spirits—and maybe this was a spirit that loved bananas. Nothing else was ever taken from the grave, even though we left other fruit. Nothing else was ever stolen or disturbed on his grave. No banana peels or other evidence of an eaten banana was ever found next to his grave or in the vicinity of his grave. And this is not a graveyard on a major road or one visited by many people. Members of that Buddhist mission are rarely seen there during the day or evening, and, anyway, no member would dare steal from a grave. Usually we are the only ones at the cemetery when we go to place flowers on the graves. We have never been able to discover what or who was taking those bananas. Perhaps it was a graveyard *obake* after all.

Carolyn Sugiyama Classen, whose story "The Spirit of Honokāne" appeared in *Hawai'i's Best Spooky Tales 2*, was born and raised in North Kohala on the Big Island and graduated from Kohala High School, the University of Hawai'i at Mānoa, and Boston College Law School. She currently divides her time between Tucson, Arizona, and Hilo, Hawai'i, doing community work in domestic violence and child abuse. She is married and has a fourteen-year-old son, Stephan Masao Classen, who also loves eating sliced bananas with peanut butter, like his late grandpa.

If you go to Lānai, you will notice how the blue sky meets the red dirt island, how little Lānai City looks like Monopoly houses all in a row, how it's so quiet and peaceful you can hear your heart beat. Enjoy the empty, rural isolation, but be on guard, always. You may begin to experience things out of the ordinary, as do the three souls in this story who insist that . . .

Something Came Between Them

There might not be much of a story if this incident happened elsewhere, in another place where strange occurrences were thought of as just that, strange occurrences.

No, this story didn't happen just any place—it happened on a tiny island in the middle of the Pacific Ocean. It happened on an island where there is a long history of roaming spirits. But who believes in spirits nowadays?

Fact is, the most famous story about the founding of this island of Lāna'i involves a young man from the neighboring island of Maui who was banished to Lāna'i for mischievous deeds in his community. He would be permitted to return only if he survived his banishment on Lāna'i, and that meant ridding the island of fearsome spirits.

Well, legend says he did just that, and today there is a large mural painted on a wall high above the lobby of the Mānele Bay Hotel celebrating the event. But are all the spirits truly gone from this peaceful island?

The three volunteers, properly known as AmeriCorps Members, were out in the field searching for sandalwood seeds. This is no easy task, since the great abundance of sandalwood trees vanished from the Hawai'i dryland forests over a century ago. There are several trees growing in the wild on Lāna'i. Some folks try to keep their location a secret so they will not be disturbed, but on this island with only 2,800 residents, there aren't many secrets.

It was a beautiful sunny day as the trio crossed the Pālāwai Basin through some abandoned pineapple fields in the old pick-up truck donated by Lānaʻi Company and headed up the dusty dirt road leading to the Munro Trail.

They pulled the truck to the side of the road when they spotted the first of the sandalwood trees. As they got out of the truck, Linda Marie took her bag, crossed the road, and climbed up the slight incline where there were several trees growing. Meanwhile, Chackleigh and Brian headed for the nearest tree, just yards from the old plantation road.

The weather was quite warm, and there was barely a breeze, which was unusual for this part of the island. As weather patterns have changed over the decades, this area was now dry, with only the few sandalwood trees, dry grasses, scattered *alaliʻi* bushes, or an occasional stunted *ʻilima*. The sandalwood tree was indeed bearing some fruit, and the fruit did contain the precious seeds the trio had come to collect.

Silently, the two men, each taking a side of the small tree, began picking off the seeds and placing them into their collection bags.

As Brian tells the rest of the story:

All of a sudden I felt as if someone had walked between us. Then I smelled a beautiful perfume scent. It was definitely a perfume fragrance, too heady for a blooming flower, and there were no flowers, no scented plants, and no breezes anywhere around. I looked over toward Chackleigh. His eyes were huge with astonishment, and he said to me, "Did you smell that?"

"Yeah!" was all I could say.

Then Chackleigh said, "Let's get out of here."

As we rushed into the road, Linda called, "What's

going on?"

We both started talking at the same time, still with chicken skin, and explained about the beautiful perfume and the feeling of someone between us. Linda, being the levelheaded, always-with-an-answer one in the group, said calmly and matter-of-factly, "Maybe it was Madame Pele."

We didn't stick around much longer. I've been back to that spot many times, even collected seeds again from that very tree, but I haven't smelled that beautiful scent, or seen Madame Pele. Yet!

Brian Valley is the Lāna'i Field Coordinator for The Nature Conservancy of Hawai'i; he manages the Kānepu'u preserve on Lāna'i, preserving and propagating Hawai'i's native plants. A native Vermonter who has lived in Hawai'i nearly a decade, he's an accomplished musician with a special "backpack" guitar that he takes out into the forest and plays for the plants. At the time of the story, Brian was an AmeriCorps member working on a joint U.S./Lāna'i Company project to protect and enhance the Lāna'i Watershed by planting Cook Island pine trees on Lāna'i Hale, the island's summit.

Originally from the East Coast, Gigi Valley moved to Maui twenty years ago. An artist and photographer, she is the public relations manager for Lāna'i Company.

Both Gigi and Brian are students of Hawaiian culture and environmental conservation and enjoy hiking, kayaking, tennis, snorkeling, scuba diving—and their island home.

Many people go to Kaua'i to see and enjoy the abundant natural beauty, but some come to retrace an old Hollywood film trail that begins at a derelict roadside hotel in the old plantation town of Kapa'a where aging fans of The King gather around a ketchup stain in the carpet, hoping they can still feel . . .

The Vibes of Elvis

Heads bowed reverently, we stand in a tight circle in the dining room of the storied Coco Palms Hotel, contemplating an antiquated, dark red, half-dollar–sized carpet stain.

"Every day during the filming of *Blue Hawaii*, Elvis would sit in this very spot and eat his cheeseburger," intones our guide, Bob Jasper. "Some people believe this is Elvis's actual ketchup stain."

One might be forgiven for believing that there is not a single inch of the island of Kaua'i—condiment splotches included—that is not imbued with some connection to a Hollywood legend. From *South Pacific* to *Jurassic Park*, the island's dazzling white beaches and emerald, waterfall-ribboned mountains have been the motion picture industry's location of choice whenever it needs a backdrop of primordial paradise.

Over the years, Kaua'i has stood in for the lush rain forest of Costa Rica, Vietnam's rice paddies, and the impenetrable African jungle—as well as Bali Hai, Fantasy Island, and Peter Pan's Never-Never Land.

Since 1933's *White Heat*, well over sixty movies have been filmed here, including *King Kong*, *The Thorn Birds*, and *Raiders of the Lost Ark*. And who could ever forget *She Gods of Shark Reef*? (Well, who besides me?) So frequent is the traffic between Hollywood and Kaua'i that

United Airlines recently took out ads in the *Los Angeles Times* touting its flights here to movie location scouts.

All this has led to a thriving spinoff business: a movie site tour. Which is what we're engaged in as we stand in the Coco Palms dining room, gazing down upon the purported Elvis stain and waiting for our goose bumps to subside.

The Coco Palms, frankly, has seen better days. Battered mercilessly by Hurricane 'Iniki in 1992, the hotel has yet to be repaired due to a longstanding legal squabble between its Singaporean owner and his insurance company. Sheets of plastic cover the bungalow roofs, and the swimming pools are empty, save for the husks of falling coconuts.

But this, more than any other site in Kaua'i, is hallowed ground for movie buffs. Security guards regularly turn away curiosity seekers, but Jasper has special permission to take his tours inside. As we stroll through the grounds, dodging the occasional dropping coconut, Jasper reels off a long list of movies filmed here: "*Miss Sadie Thompson, Bird of Paradise, Jungle Heat, Naked Paradise . . .* "

Nobody's listening. There's only one film worth talking about here: *Blue Hawaii.* This is what brought Judy Boggs of Snow Camp, N.C., on the Hawai'i Movie Tour. This is what brought her to Kaua'i, and this is what brought her to the Hawaiian Islands for her first and perhaps only visit.

"I begged my husband to come so we could renew our wedding vows on the wedding raft like Elvis," Boggs tells me, "but I couldn't get him on the plane."

Instead, she has come with her friend, Irene Smith of Denver, who, as we shall see later, has her own agenda. Boggs and Smith were so determined to take the movie tour that when they learned there were no openings during their visit they changed their flight and stayed in Kaua'i an extra day.

Jasper points across an artificial lagoon to the bungalow on the end. "Right there, that one was Elvis's bungalow," he says. He shows us the palm trees planted by Jackie Kennedy and Bing Crosby (they have plaques). Elvis never got around to planting one.

"I've worn out two copies of *Blue Hawaii* on video," Boggs confides to me. "My husband always picks at me, telling me I live in fantasy, not reality. But I always said that one day I'm going to go there. And now I'm here."

Jasper leads us inside to the palm-fringed bar, to the very spot where Elvis leaned in one scene. "If you want to feel the vibes of Elvis," he says, "lean here."

Boggs, who doesn't need to be told where Elvis stood in the film, leans against the bar and has her friend Smith snap her picture.

We move into the Lagoon Dining Room, and Jasper explains how Elvis sat at the same corner table every day, ordering bacon and eggs for breakfast, a cheeseburger for lunch, and another cheeseburger for dinner. Sometimes when the restaurant got busy, Jasper says, the future King would jump up and bus tables, to the great amusement of hotel guests. He launches into another story about Elvis engaging in some chauvinistic behavior, but Boggs interrupts.

"Every man," she says with a smile, "should take lessons from Elvis."

Once we've all inspected the alleged Elvis ketchup stain, we move over to the long, open window overlooking the lagoon. Parked at one end is the wedding raft—a platform spanning two outrigger canoes—that bore Elvis and his bride in one of the most memorable scenes in *Blue*

Hawaii. It is available for real weddings, and perhaps one day Boggs will renew her vows here—if her husband back in North Carolina ever gets in touch with his inner Elvis.

John Flinn is the travel editor of the *San Francisco Examiner*, where this story first appeared. An Elvis fan who's also visited Graceland, he is a frequent visitor to Hawai'i.

Night Visitors

Midnight Haircut in Kalihi

The Ghost in the Wall

Impressions of Lanaʻi

Dream or Ghost at Kaunolū?

A Ghostly Tribe

The Graveyard Shift at ʻEwa

One day I asked a pal in San Francisco if anything unusual had ever happened to him in his time Hawai'i. "No," he said, "I'm too pragmatic and insensitive to things of that nature." But that night when he asked his Filipina wife, who grew up in Kalihi, the same question, her eyes grew big and wide and her hair stood on end, and she told him this story about her . . .

Midnight Haircut in Kalihi

One night in 1991, while I was spending the weekend at my parents' home on Auld Lane in Kalihi, the strangest thing happened to me. I can never forget.

I was sleeping in my old childhood bedroom and don't remember anything unusual about that night, no dreams or nightmares, just a good night's sleep in the safe comfort of my family home.

But when I woke up and was taking a shower I noticed that my neck seemed to be shaved, or cut close, about two inches all around, the hair taken off during the night from the nape of my neck on up.

I asked my sister, Imelda, who had slept in the room with me, if she had cut my hair during the night. Maybe it was just a sister's prank.

She was surprised and shocked that I would even think to ask, but she was also amazed to see that my hair was cut so close and evenly.

Yet there was no hair on my bed or anywhere in the house. How could my hair have been cut—and where were the trimmings?

I was really spooked.

I told my mom about it and she said, casually, "Oh yes, the Kaibaan were here during the night; they must have cut your hair."

"What?" I demanded.

"Oh, sure," she said, "the Kaibaan must have paid you a visit while you slept. It happens all the time in the Philippines. The Kaibaan ("little guys" in Filipino) travel in a gang, and either use their teeth or scissors to cut human hair.

"They walk backward, only come out on dark nights, and are scared of rosaries and the Cross of Jesus."

I showed my neck to my cousin and a neighbor, and they all agreed it was the Kaibaan, for they were familiar with them from the Philippines as well.

Nothing like that had ever happened to me, and hasn't since, thank goodness. It gives me chicken skin now just to think about it.

It took about one year for that part of my hair to grow back to match the rest of my hair.

I live near San Francisco now and sometimes I wonder: will they come here, or are they unique to Hawai'i and the Philippines?

My grandfather once told me that even stranger things happen in Hawai'i than in the Philippines; he says the energy in Hawai'i is stronger.

Maria de Leon was born in the Philippines and immigrated to the United States during her teen years. She grew up in Kalihi and now lives in the Bay Area.

Scritch scritch scritch. What's that sound? A ghost, a wandering spirit? An entire family in windward Oʻahu wakes in the middle of the night to hear something in the wall of their house. In this chilling, often humorous story of a midnight encounter in Maunawili, author Steve Heller tells how his wife and three sons try in various ways to deal with the nightmare of . . .

The Ghost in the Wall

We'd all heard the noises in the middle of the night: faint scratching sounds in the wall of our rented house on the edge of the lush tropical forest of Maunawili on the windward side of Oʻahu. The forest was full of spirits, our neighbors said, and we believed them. At one time or another, each of us had heard strange sounds echo from the green depths of the *koa*, guava, and *kukui* trees. Mournful sounds like the wailing of lost, wandering souls. But the sounds in the walls of our house were different: like fingernails clawing on the other side of the wood paneling. Like someone trying to tear and scratch his way out.

"Maybe it's a ghost," David, our thirteen-year-old, suggested at breakfast the morning after the sounds began to haunt us. He stared straight at our first-grader, Daniel.

"No way!" Daniel replied. "Ghosts don't sound like that."

I laid down the sports page of the *Honolulu Advertiser*. All of us were groggy from lack of sleep. "How do ghosts sound?"

"Ghosts go 'wooooooo, wooooooOOOOOOO!' Then they come get you in your bed."

"Maybe it'll get you tonight," Michael, our middle child, suggested as he poured milk over his Cheerios.

Daniel's eyes widened.

"Stop trying to scare your brother," Mary said from the kitchen.

"It's probably just a mouse messing around in the insulation between the walls," I replied. "Nothing to worry about."

"Maybe it's a Hawaiian ghost," David said. "The kind Dad writes about that used to live on Lāna'i." He looked at Daniel again and arched an eyebrow. "A man-eater."

"Stop that," I instructed David. "Whatever it is, it won't hurt us."

"That's easy for you to say, Dad," Michael chimed in. "You sleep through everything."

It's true. When the clawing sound had wakened every- one else at 2 a.m., Mary had to punch me in the side. Get up and see what it is. After a brief inspection, I located the general source of the sound: the wall between the master bedroom and the room where Michael and Daniel slept. The scratching was faint, but distinct. And persistent. Whatever was in there knew what it was doing. When I tapped on the wall, the scratching stopped. Go back to bed, I finally ordered everyone. It's no big deal.

Later in the night, the scratching sound returned, waking the boys from dreams of ghosts and goblins. When David wanted to wake me again with the news, Mary told him it would keep till morning.

Daniel pushed away his cereal bowl. "I don't want a ghost in the wall."

"There's no ghost," I promised. "But if you hear it again tonight, wake me and I'll take care of it."

Michael shook his head as he scooped the last of his Cheerios onto his spoon. "Sure, Dad. Like that's going to happen."

That night I dreamed I saw an enormous man-eating ghost, just like the one who chased Prince Kaululā'au down the mountainside on Lāna'i five centuries ago. The ghost loomed up out of nowhere and seized me by the throat. No! You've got the wrong man! I started to cry out—when I opened my eyes and discovered Mary shaking me by my shoulders.

"Get up!" she insisted. "That thing is coming out of the wall!"

"What do you mean 'coming out'?"

Suddenly, Michael and Daniel were beside the bed. "It's eating its way out," Michael said.

I sat up on my elbows. "Where?"

"Right above the baseboard behind my bed," Daniel said. He was trembling.

I laid a hand on his shoulder. "Nothing's going to eat you." I turned toward Michael again as I swung my legs off the bed. "And nothing's eating its way through the wall."

"But Dad," Michael insisted, the thrill of impending doom rising in his voice. "I can see its nose!"

Ten seconds later I could see it too: poking right through the beige wood paneling in the yellow light of Michael's desk lamp, sniffing the air like a desert wanderer catching his first whiff of the sea.

The rest of the family huddled just inside the doorway behind me. "What is it?" Daniel demanded.

"Not a ghost," I said. "Looks like our backyard friend: the rat."

"Oh God, Steve," Mary cried out, "get rid of that thing!"

Get rid of it? Each of us had seen the rat many times, all four pounds of him, climbing up and down the sloping silver-ringed trunk of the coco palm next to the chain-link fence that separated our backyard from the dense forest.

Apparently the rat had made his nest among the ripening olive green coconuts at the very top of the tree. Now that he'd decided to move indoors, what was I supposed to do about it?

Daniel knew: "Save us, Dad!"

"Maybe you can scare him," David suggested in a calmer voice, as he peered around his mother's backside from the hallway. David didn't want to be left out of whatever was going to happen—but the nose poking through the wall frightened him as much as anyone.

Then I did one of those father things the boys will probably never forget.

"Michael, hand me your sneaker."

I waited until the twitchy gray nose thrust itself as far through the wood as the hole would allow—then BAMN!

When I pulled back the heel of the sneaker, only the hole remained. An instant later we all heard a scuffling sound move quickly along the baseboard toward the exterior wall of the house—then nothing.

"Is it gone?" Daniel asked breathlessly. "Are we safe?"

I smiled back at him. "For the moment."

"Wow, Dad," Michael said. "You're bad."

I duct-taped a brick over the hole, then sent everyone to bed.

"You sure that'll keep the rat out?" Daniel asked, as he crawled under his covers.

"For tonight, at least. Now get some sleep."

No one heard anything further from the rat that evening. In the morning we all searched for the intruder's secret entrance to the house but found nothing.

"We've got to do something," Mary insisted. "We can't live with an animal that eats through walls."

"We won't have to," I replied. A few minutes later I

took a screwdriver and widened the hole just enough to stuff it with rat poison, then retaped the brick. Then I set more poison on a plate in the backyard near the trunk of the coco palm, covering the plate with a newspaper weighted by a rock, so the spotted doves and Japanese white-eyes we all loved wouldn't eat it.

David looked down at the trap and frowned. "You sure this'll work?"

"We'll see."

Each morning after that, I lifted the newspaper and checked the plate. Each morning a little more of the poison had vanished. We saw no other sign of the rat, but every night scratching, gnawing sounds continued to emanate from the interior walls of the house—a different wall every night. Tap, tap, scritch, scritch. The rat was building a tenement complex inside our home. Now even I couldn't sleep.

"I can't stand this," Mary moaned one evening shortly after midnight. Scritch, pick, pick. The rat was carving a decorative sculpture somewhere behind our dresser. "Tomorrow morning I want you to call an exterminator."

"Let's give it one more night," I pleaded.

The next night the walls were quiet. I was certain because I'd lain awake most of the night, listening.

"What if the rat died inside a wall?" Daniel asked the following morning.

David gave him a grave look over a half-eaten Eggo waffle. "It'll come back as a ghost and haunt this house forever."

"You mean stink up the house forever," Michael countered.

Daniel turned to me and frowned. "I don't want that."

Dizzy from lack of sleep, I wasn't sure which type of

haunting worried me the most. But what could I do about either? Then, an hour later that same morning, our luck changed. Michael found the dead, bloated rat near the back fence.

"What are we going to do with the body?" Daniel asked as we gathered round it.

"Rat stew," David suggested.

"Maybe you should bury it," Mary suggested.

"I've got a better idea." The rest of the family stood by as I went to the carport and returned with a pair of work gloves. I picked up the rat with one hand and held it out at arm's length.

"Depart this place, you evil spirit!" I said to the rat— then hurled it high over the chain-link fence into the enchanted forest of Maunawili.

When I turned back around, Michael shook his head. "Dad, you're so bad, you're nearly rad."

"Goodbye, rat," Daniel said, and waved at the trees.

That night the forest moaned and shrieked with the pleadings of another lost soul. The Hellers all slept soundly till morning.

Steve Heller is a professor of creative writing at Kansas State University's Department of English and the author of *The Ghost Killer: New and Selected Stories of Hawai'i*. He is now writing *Private Island*, a narrative history of Lāna'i. Heller also contributed "Missing Man" on page 91.

It was new and different, an upland lodge in the cool, cloud-wreathed pine forest of a remote Hawaiian Island, and curiosity ran high, especially in the tourism industry, when The Lodge at Kō'ele opened on Lāna'i a few years ago. A Canadian hotel executive accepts an invitation to spend the weekend at The Lodge and finds her experiences go far beyond the usual . . .

Impressions of Lāna'i

I remember being very excited at the invitation to tour the newly opened Lodge at Kō'ele on the island of Lāna'i. At the time, I was working at a luxury resort in Wailea, Maui, and speculation about this new "hunting lodge" hotel was running high. I couldn't wait to experience it myself!

The weekend started perfectly—a short flight to Lāna'i, the lazy scenic drive up the old volcanic mountain, an elegant sense of arrival in The Great Hall.

My room, with its cozy window seat and flowered curtains, faced the forest and orchid conservatory. Deer grazed on the spacious green lawns, and the air, scented with Norfolk Island pine, was cool and moist.

We spent the day in exploration: fabulously appointed butler suites, the eclectic furnishings of The Great Hall, a warmly appointed cocktail lounge sporting colorful clusters of glass fruit, buttery soft leather chairs in the extensive library.

Following a fabulous dinner of locally raised venison and fresh island vegetables accompanied by a couple of glasses of fine wine, I was thoroughly relaxed, and after socializing in the lounge for a while, I was ready to retire for the night.

Because we were sharing accommodations, I was to sleep in the Murphy bed. It was large and comfortable and cozy, and I was looking forward to a restful night and another exciting day.

After a sleepy chat reliving the day and speculating about the next one, I drifted off to dreamland. The night was cool and dark and very, very quiet. Until I awoke in terror.

For a minute or two I couldn't figure out whether it was a nightmare or if it was actually happening—a terrible, terrible weight on my chest, and a pervasive sense of anger.

Someone—or something—was clearly very unhappy with finding me in this place where I obviously didn't belong. Never before, nor since, have I felt such terror or personal danger! I could see nothing but blackness—no stars, no light seeping under the door, nothing.

I tried to call out, but was unable to make a sound — and this oppressive weight had me pinned, paralyzed, against the mattress.

Breathing was difficult. I lost all sense of time, and at some point must have passed out. When consciousness returned, the weight and the angry presence were still there, only now there was also the sensation of being "pushed."

I have no idea how long this continued, and then, suddenly, there was the sensation of something actually pushing its way right through my body. This seems impossible, and yet the feeling was unmistakable.

The relief was immediate, and while there was no hope in the world of falling back to sleep, the weight, the anger, and the pervasive blackness were gone.

My girlfriend saw me the next morning and said, "You look like hell. What happened to you?"

I told her, but she was incredulous.

Most people are, even today.

I know it sounds wild and unbelievable, and yet I also know it happened. I have since learned that this was no isolated incident—that there have been several similar "experiences" at The Lodge at Kō'ele. I know I'm not the only one, only one of the first.

People born in the Islands apparently do not receive these visitations—I was born in Canada—and it has been suggested that a light left on in the hotel room may discourage the spirits from entering.

Some say The Lodge is built in the path of the night marchers. Others attribute the spirit visitations to the relocation of a small church, which now stands just off to one side of the resort.

Whatever the case, that was one weekend that definitely left a lasting impression.

People since have asked if I would ever stay at The Lodge again. Absolutely yes. Only this time I'd take the advice of Tom Bodette of Motel 6 fame, and "leave a light on for ya?"

Ann Donohue moved to Maui from Vancouver, Canada, in 1981. Her 10-plus years in the hotel and hospitality industry encompass sales, marketing, and public relations management. Ann and her two dogs reside in Kula, on the slopes of Haleakalā.

One night a woman fell asleep near King Kamehameha's house at the royal fishing village, which is still full of *mana*, and experienced the strangest visitation. To this day she wonders was it a . . .

Dream or Ghost at Kaunolū?

We went down in the late afternoon, down the long hard dusty road to Kaunolū, an ancient Hawaiian village. It's a place with plenty of *mana*; used to be a place of refuge and there is a big *heiau*, lots of old house sites, and a place that is said to be where King Kamehameha lived when he came to Lānaʻi to celebrate the Makahiki.

Well, we parked the Jeep just under the old *keawe* tree that grows right there where Kamehameha had his house; and my friend went down the cliff and over the streambed to go night fishing. I watched the glow from his gaslight disappear around the side of the cliff and lay back in the bed of the Jeep. We had a mattress there and it was comfortable, but a little spooky because that place always is— a little spooky.

I guess I fell asleep.

I think I woke up and I was lying in the Jeep under the tree, but it was different somehow. I felt like I was dreaming, but if I was, it was a dream about me being right there, just where I was. There was a man standing by the tailgate of the Jeep and he looked kind of old-fashioned. He was tall and skinny and had a badge on, like the kind of badges sheriffs wore in Western movies. He was telling me that he was looking for a man who had murdered someone there, and I should be careful. I can't remember the exact thing about it, but it was some "local" guy who was wanted for this murder and I got kind of nervous and worried. Then the man wasn't there anymore and I was still lying in the Jeep and I decided that I had been dreaming. But I was restless all night.

I might have told the story to some people over the years, but it just seemed like a peculiar dream, because when you dream about being in the same place you are when you are dreaming, it feels kind of funny. Is it really a dream?

A long time later I was with my friend, Moana, and we were talking about Kaunolū, because her great-great-uncle, Ohua, was the last Hawaiian man to live at Kaunolū. Ohua was some kind of *kahu* of the place and took care of hiding the last known carved god on Lāna'i. His brother, Keali'ihananui, was the last Hawaiian to live in the Pālāwai Basin.

I told her about my dream, and she said, "That's funny, because my great-great-grandfather, Keali'ihananui, was a sheriff, and he was looking for a murderer; maybe he went down to Kaunolū to ask his brother about it."

So, I don't know, was it a dream or was it a ghost?

Joana McIntyre Varawa is the author of three books: *Mind in the Waters*, *The Delicate Art of Whale Watching*, and *Changes in Latitude*, and is currently working on a fourth, *Animal Spirit/Animal Soul*. Her work has appeared on radio and in newspapers and magazines, and in *Travelers' Tales Hawaii*. Formerly of San Francisco, where she founded Project Jonah to secure a moratorium on commercial whaling, Varawa has lived on the island of Lāna'i since 1976; she is the editor of *The Lāna'i Times*.

Visitors often wake up jet-lagged in Waikīkī. They get up in the middle of the night and go out on their hotel lanai to savor the balmy night air, enjoy the trade winds and see, many for the first time, the moon and stars above the Pacific. Sometimes they get a chill in the tropic night; think they hear and see people who aren't really there. Or are they? Something like that happened to this young man, who woke one night to witness a woman's grisly encounter with . . .

A Ghostly Tribe

Once when I lived in Hawai'i I had the most terrifying experience. My mom, Nana, and I went to visit my uncle in Honolulu. He didn't have enough room for everyone, so, stupid me said, "Let's just go to Outrigger." So we did.

At 12:38 a.m. I woke up. I went out on the balcony and just sat on a chair, then went to sleep again.

The next morning I got a stunning chill. I saw a woman. She was really pretty, but looked sad. She didn't say anything except "They're coming." And then she just disappeared.

The next night I got up again around 12:40 and saw outside one hundred men, all of them gathered and chanting a weird chant. Then I saw a woman. She looked at me. It was the woman I had seen the night before. She was crying. Then I just fell down crying. I felt her fear. It was terrifying. Then I saw the gruesome death of that woman. I just blacked out. I wish I could have saved her.

Michael Hocker, born in Hawai'i but now living in McAllen, Texas, would like to be a writer one day. He has written a lot of stories—twenty so far—but this one is true.

When you work on a Hawai'i sugar plantation, one day is much like the next—cut cane, haul cane, process cane into sugar. Once in a while, though, something extraordinary occurs, as Simon Nasario reveals in a classic plantation-era story about what happened to him on . . .

The Graveyard Shift at 'Ewa

I worked for the 'Ewa Sugar Company as a tractor serviceman on the three p.m. to midnight shift. This incident happened close to the end of the shift, around midnight.

The night this happened was one of those real damp, misty, foggy nights in 1988, during one of the winter months.

My job was to go to wherever tractors were working and service them. Work consisted of changing air filters and greasing the boggie wheels and cable winches.

This particular night I went to service a tractor that was plowing a field next to the graveyard. This graveyard is located just before you turn off the 'Ewa Beach Road to go to the main part of the sugar company.

'Most all the bodies buried at the graveyard in 'Ewa were buried in wooden boxes made by the plantation, so boxes rotted out fast in the ground. My dad and my uncle are buried there.

The swamper (helper) to the tractor operator was a Filipino boy by the name of Juanito De la Cruz. His job was to ride the plow and adjust the heights of the plow discs when needed.

The night was real dark, no stars were out, and it was cold, damp, and drizzling a fine mist of rain. As I neared the fence of the graveyard, I noticed that it looked like a scene from a horror movie that takes place in a swamp.

There was a bluish glow hovering about a foot above the ground and moving up and down and along the ground in places.

I flashed the lights of my truck at the fellow operating the tractor to come to where I was parked.

When he got to where I was, I called De la Cruz's attention to the phenomenon in the graveyard. He asked me what that was, so I told him that it was the spirits of all the dead people in their graves trying to get to heaven.

Poor old De La Cruz got so scared that he jumped off the plow and ran home. The next night he asked to be assigned to work elsewhere, as long as it wasn't anywhere near the graveyard.

Juanito De La Cruz served with me in D Company of the 298th Infantry during World War II. I always kidded him about that night.

Years later, a teacher friend of mine explained to me that the glow in the graveyard was some kind of gas from the decomposing bodies coming up through the ground and mixing with the fine mist that was present.

I didn't know whether to believe him or not. I still think it was some spirit thing.

Simon Nasario was born in 'Ewa, O'ahu, where he also attended grade school. A 1938 graduate of McKinley High School, he served with D Company, 298th Infantry, from November 1941 to November 1945. A former worker at 'Ewa Plantation, he now lives on the mainland. Nasario also contributed "The Spirit of the Shade Tree" on page 48.

Nature and Spirits

Missing Man

Listen to the Wind

On the Wettest Spot on Earth

The upland rain forests of O'ahu look friendly and inviting; you think, "I'll just park the car at the scenic lookout and take a walk in the woods," little realizing that Hawai'i forests are deceptive; they are "a green unknown," a kind of no-man's land. Each year hundreds of hikers enter the forest, many stray off the established trail, a few never return, like the . . .

Missing Man

In late June of 1995, a hiker disappeared in the dense tropical forest of Maunawili on the windward side of the Hawaiian island of Oʻahu. His name was Tim Pantaleoni. He was traveling alone, staying in a small bed-and-breakfast owned and operated by the mother of my friend and colleague, the writer Robert Onopa.

When the young man failed to return twenty-four hours after announcing his intention to hike the trail cut through the forest along the base of the curving jagged green cliffs of the Koʻolau Mountains, Bob and a number of other volunteers set out to look for him. The forest of Maunawili is the wettest, most densely foliaged area on Oʻahu. It is not to be trifled with. Do not leave the trail, the guidebooks warn. Do not set off on your own. When Tim Pantaleoni's rusty ten-speed bike was found leaning against a chain-link fence surrounding a water tank near one of the trailheads, the Honolulu County Search and Rescue Team was contacted. Within an hour, a yellow helicopter began to spiral in an ever-widening circle above the deep green bowl of Maunawili.

My wife and our three boys watched the helicopter from the backyard of our comfortable four-bedroom house on a quiet street at the edge of the forest. I had just finished my semester as Visiting Writer at the state university on the other side of the mountains, and we were staying on through the summer before returning to Kansas. The chain-link fence behind our house appeared to restrain the wilderness, holding back the grasping branches of *koa*, monkeypod, Hawaiian mountain apple trees, and *uluhe* ferns. The opposite was actually true: The Maunawili subdivision advances farther into the forest each year, giant earth-moving machines eating their way through the lush greenery toward the looming mountain. For the present, though, the forest remains large and dangerous. This was the fourth time in six months we had watched the same search helicopter circle the valley. The boys were used to it now.

"Why do those fools have to leave the trail?" David, our oldest, asked as we watched the 'copter make another slow loop toward the mountain.

"You know haoles," our middle son, Michael, the cynical wit, replied. "You can't teach 'em anything."

Everyone laughed except our first-grader, Daniel, whose attention remained fixed on the 'copter inching away from us across the blue ceiling of the valley, the nick-nick-nick of its rotating blades slowly fading. Beneath the nicking sound I could feel the forest breathing. "They're not gonna find him," Daniel said, and the rest of us fell silent.

Three days later the 'copter was still circling overhead. Our neighbors advised me against joining the daily group of volunteer ground searchers. "You'll just get in the way," the shopkeeper who lived across the street informed me. "He's obviously not on the trail, and if you leave the trail to look for him, they'll just have to come look for you." Nevertheless, shortly after sunrise that same morning, I joined a small group at the trailhead at the top of Lopaka Street, where Tim Pantaleoni's bike had been found. By the middle of the afternoon, I was trudging back down from the trailhead through the streets of the Maunawili subdivision. The shopkeeper was right: I was useless.

By this time Tim Pantaleoni's mother had arrived from the mainland, posting yellow flyers on every telephone pole and fence post I passed on the long, discouraging walk home. In large bold letters the flyers proclaimed: MISS-ING MAN. Beneath the letters was a photocopied picture of a thin-faced, determined-looking young man in his early thirties. Something about the image immediately haunted me. It brought to mind something I couldn't identify, until all at once it hit me: The missing man looked like my father. My father as I never actually saw him in the flesh, my father as I've seen him only in faded black-and-white pictures my mother keeps in a stack of thick yellowed envelopes in a desk in her apartment in Manhattan, Kansas.

One image, in particular, came to mind: PFC Steve Heller, Sr., in his mustering-out uniform, just back from the Second World War, khaki tie tucked neatly into his uniform shirt. He is leaning against the driver's side of a 1939 Mercury convertible with white sidewalls, his left arm draped over the base of the open window, his right fist braced on his hip just below his regulation khaki belt.

His body language is jaunty, cocky. Everything life has to offer is within his reach, and he will have everything he can grasp. Behind him stretches the dusty, unpaved path of Fairmont Street climbing Mulligan's Bluff in Kansas City, Missouri. This is the street Father grew up on, but the truth is, he would never travel this path again. A minute after Mother took this picture, they climbed back into the Mercury, and Father turned off Fairmont onto a side street and left Kansas City for good, choosing to seek their future by a new path. The paths Father chose weren't really paths, but gambles. Whenever the trail became too familiar, he would leave it. In the almost half-century that followed the photograph, Father would hold at least fifty different blue-collar jobs, ranging from janitor to electrician. Twice, he would go into business for himself. He would win and lose a small fortune. He would attain, then lose, his life's dream of owning his own garage and auto-body shop. Throughout his life, he would ignore advice that might have served him well, preferring always to go his own way. And he would always keep going, no matter what, through an amazing array of injuries and illnesses: a twice-broken back, broken arms and legs, ulcers, diabetes, heart disease, a series of devastating strokes, and, near the end, the beginnings of Parkinson's syndrome. Through all these things, he always worked to provide for my mother Elizabeth and me. Though his decisions were often quirky or hardheaded, they were never selfish. Mother and I always came first.

On Kamehameha Day, a couple of weeks before Tim Pantaleoni disappeared, Mother had called from Kansas with the news that Dad had died in his room in the health care wing of Meadow Lark Hills Retirement Community. "He was in no pain," Mother explained. "His body just gave out."

No pain. That sounded like a path Father would have never chosen willingly. The one supposedly pain-free path he always claimed he wanted to take before he died would have brought him right here, to Hawai'i, which he had never seen except through my eyes. He and Mother intended to fly out and visit us in Maunawili at the end of the summer, just in time for their fiftieth wedding anniversary. Now he would make the trip one day ahead of Mother, in a plastic bag sealed inside a vinyl box the size of a small purse.

Prior to Mother's arrival, I loaded Mary and the boys into our rented Nissan and drove down to the golden sand that encloses Kailua Bay, into which the heavy rains of Maunawili drain.

On the edge of the sea, I gathered my family around me and constructed a ceremony that mimicked the ritual my mother and I would later enact—just the two of us—for in her grief that is how she preferred it, on this same beach on a windswept morning exactly one week later, as the sun spackled the eastern sky gold and green above the azure blue sea.

I scooped up a handful of dry sand, then instructed Mary and the boys to do the same.

"These grains of sand in our palms represent the spirit of your Grandpa Heller," I told David, Michael, and Daniel. "Grandpa loved life, but life was never easy for him. He wanted everything life had to offer, but he didn't really want if for himself. He wanted it for your grandma, for me, and finally for you. He worked hard and made many sacrifices. If he hadn't done these things, I never would have gone to college. And your mother and I probably never could have made the life for us that we've all enjoyed so far."

"That's right," Mary said.

We joined our free hands and I led everyone into the gently lapping water, up to my knees.

"Grandpa always went his own way in life. Now we're gong to lower our palms into the sea and release Grandpa's spirit, so it can go wherever it wants to go."

Without another word, we lowered our palms into the undulating blue water and watched the grains darken, disperse, then disappear.

I never met Tim Pantaleoni and don't know what kind of man he was. Nevertheless, through the images of my father that I carry in my head, I can't help but imagine the life he might have lived. At the time of his disappearance, he was thirty-three, the age my father was when I was born, when the future was a bewildering maze of choices, a labyrinth of possible paths.

Tim Pantaleoni was never found. I like to think his spirit endures in the green depths of Maunawili, wandering through the tangled web of the living, breathing forest, occasionally crossing the trail, where an alert hiker might catch a glimpse of him, if the light is just right.

And on hot, sultry days, when the blazing tropical sun lifts moisture from Kailua Bay and the trade winds carry it inland to the mountains, filling the vast green bowl of the valley with a steamy mist, I picture the spirit of my father moving simultaneously through the same dense forest, never following the established trail, hiking even deeper into the green unknown, examining each leaf and stone with the seasoned vision of the experienced searcher, missing nothing.

Steve Heller is a professor of creative writing at Kansas State University's Department of English and the author of *The Ghost Killer: New and Selected Stories of Hawai'i.* He is now writing "Private Island," a narrative history of Lāna'i. His story "Missing Man" is part of "The Book of Roy," a collection of narrative essays about his life and family. "Missing Man" will be published soon in a British journal called *Birdsuit.* Heller also contributed "The Ghost in the Wall" on page 70.

In Hawai'i, you would have to be deeply estranged from the natural world not to feel the life in this land, in this 'āina. It's everywhere around us in contrasting tones of soothing beauty and raw power—from rain-drenched valleys to Pele's scorching lava flows, to isolated places where you can . . .

Listen to the Wind

I was one of those people seeking the sacred in nature, slipping past the end of the trail, reaching for the untrampled and the wild. Drawn here, called by the siren song of living land and clean, warm seas, where animals are family gods, and goddesses sculpt with waterfalls and lava, I relocated my family from the bustle of California to find the sacred natural and peace. I fell so deeply into Maui's green arms that I felt compelled to share my reverence with others.

And so it was no surprise that I found myself co-leading adventure journeys with groups of women dedicated to self-growth and a healthy appreciation for the great out-of-doors. We traveled to places off the beaten trail, private lands where we were guests and public lands that were sufficiently remote; open seas we shared with whales.

Every journey was extraordinary, every destination as complex and magical as every woman who participated. But it was on Moloka'i that some of us shared an event that stands out as an epiphany, one that reminded me that all of us are able to access the sacred in nature, but that we must listen to nature's voice, and silence our own.

Our group of seven had spent the day bathing in mud pools, hiking in Hālawa Valley (it is now closed to the public), conducting personal ceremonies, and talking. Every person has a story to share. The inner journey turned outward is an integral part of the growth experience. But sometimes, sharing in conversation crosses over to just plain talking . . . and talking. And it was the talking that began to concern me.

I have led many trips to many wondrous places only to have them marred by the incessant chatter that people can get lost in. And so often the chatter revolves around the world that people have rushed to leave behind. Or it involves the comparison game: "This place looks just like this other place I visited . . . "

Once in a while, we humans are humbled by nature's voice. Nature thunders, she storms and she rages; she can silence our chatter. But also, she whispers, she rustles, she sighs, and we cannot hear this voice if our own is too loud.

That night, at the end of a cozy campfire, when the darkness began to silence the world, I was inspired to call for twelve hours of silence for our group. Each one of us was left to face our own inner voices, to finally face the next step that we had pledged to take.

It was precisely at the end of our self-imposed silence the next morning when the wind gusted through our campsite with such force that it caught my attention.

I watched in horror as a dead palm frond tore loose from a towering palm on the edge of our group and came crashing down onto a tent. As I headed for the tent, I passed a trip participant who was trying to shake a trespassing centipede from her lap without screaming (being a seriously dedicated student of silence). My wish that no one was inside the crumpled tent went unfulfilled as our friend Jen staggered out holding a bloody towel to her face.

We swarmed around her like bees, trying to diagnose, attempting to help. Aside from her broken nose, there were no other injuries, and the palm frond had hit her dead on. Jen was a nurse. She chose not to be transported to the hospital but to allow our deeply connected group to assist her in her own healing techniques. We followed her willingness to heal herself with loving support and first aid, focused attention and our host's *ho'oponopono* (purifying) ministrations.

She told us that moments before the palm frond had hit her, she had been praying for a message from God. Jen is also a cancer survivor. She already knew how to heal herself, had faced what our culture views as the scariest harbinger of doom, but doubting herself, she was given another opportunity. She got the message. And now she looks for softer messages, she listens very carefully. She spends a lot of time in nature, and she is very healthy. And her nose healed perfectly.

I am listening a lot more carefully these days, too. I treasure these islands of rainbow rain, with reefs like cathedrals and the wisdom of the host culture. Sometimes still, another person who hears what I do not has to step in and remind me to cut my own chatter.

I fully appreciate the concern many *kama'āina* have for the sanctity of this sacred natural world. Too many people coming into delicately balanced ecosystems, chattering too much about the world they long to leave behind, can drown out nature's voice. We must "listen to the forest" as Eddie Kamae says, and listen to our own bodies for nature's most important messages.

Hannah Bernard lives with her family not too far from the ocean on one of Haleakalā's green flanks. Her day job as director of the nonprofit Hawai'i Wildlife Fund consists of leading snorkel and whale-watch trips, conducting endangered species recovery research, and actively campaigning for the protection of wilderness.

You can hike a long, steep, muddy footpath to the nearly mile-high summit of Mt. Wai'ale'ale, or fly over the spiky cloud-wreathed caldera in a helicopter. Only a few people I know have spent the night near the *heiau* of Wai'ale'ale, and been lost in the clouds . . .

On the Wettest Spot in the World

The Hawaiians left more than just stories and ghosts on Kaua'i—they left tangible things: temples, house platforms, and terraces. Of sensible design to begin with, they're in disrepair now, their edges and angles often worn by time and weather. There is nothing in them out of harmony with the land, and coming upon one while walking on Kaua'i is one of the fascinations of the island.

There is one temple, on Mount Wai'ale'ale, that still receives offerings. I camped near it several years ago, eager to try out a new tent I had bought in a mountain shop on the mainland. Wai'ale'ale, the rainiest place on earth, would be the ultimate test for my tent.

Visitors to the summit of Wai'ale'ale usually use Keaku cave for shelter, and I ate dinner there, but the cave is always cold and damp, and I was happy to brave the rain and pitch my tent.

I crawled in for a cozy night, listening to the rain splattering lightly against the cotton tent walls, confident that I was camping in as wet a place as anybody had ever camped in before. I listened as the rain increased in intensity, and felt around anxiously for any leaks. The rain falling on the taut sides became louder and louder. The tent was soon like the inside of a bass drum. The noise became almost unbearable, but I was not about to leave the tent, and although I did not have a moment's sleep that night, not a drop of water entered the tent.

Near where I pitched camp on the summit, the Wainiha River, which flows into the Pacific Ocean on the north shore, has its source in a small lake. Held sacred by the early Hawaiians, it is hardly a real lake, only thirty feet in diameter and two feet deep in a rainstorm, which is almost always. The lake bottom is composed of small pebbles and sand, and the water is clear, in contrast to the surrounding muck and stubby grass. Near the lake is a small temple platform of hand-fitted rock about ten feet square. It is the *heiau* of Waiʻaleʻale, to which the Hawaiians of all classes once toiled from Hanalei and Waimea to pay homage to the gods of the woods and the mountains.

That morning I walked toward the temple. The wet earth around the *heiau* platform sparkled with shiny dimes and nickels scattered there—present-day offerings still made to the gods of the mountain. Amazed at my own stupidity, I realized that I had forgotten to make my offerings the night before. Fortunately, the gods of Waiʻaleʻale were not as powerful that night as they once had been, and they only deprived me of my sleep.

The head gods of the mountain, like the Hāʻena dragon, may have departed in disgust, but Waiʻaleʻale still dominates the island. For me it has always been, even more than the Alakaʻi Swamp, the most fascinating place on Kauaʻi. Nowhere in the world is weather—the primeval power of cloud and rain—so dramatically on display. Camping on Waiʻaleʻale is an experience like no other—not even approached in the Cascades of the Northwest or in any other wet place in the continental United States.

Keaku Cave is the only dry place within a dozen miles of Waiʻaleʻale. Perched high on the side of a clay cliff near a small stream that lower down becomes the Olokele

River, the small cave, not high enough for a standing five-footer, is deep enough to stretch out in, though tenants must roll up their sleeping bags to cook dinner. The cave is one mile and three hours from the Wai'ale'ale summit, which, though it is not the highest point on the mountain, is the most comfortable high point. Kawaikini Peak, ninety feet higher and three-fifths of a mile south, is too small and slippery to stand on.

The small stream is a hundred feet below the cave, but water needs are easily satisfied. We held a pan outside the cave entrance into the steady rain and filled it up in minutes with fresh, cold water, Far back in a dark corner of the cave is a crumbling wood calabash, undoubtedly brought here by a Hawaiian many years ago. We once found a rusting ship's lantern resting on the smooth, worn surface of the cave floor, but it fell into small pieces when we picked it up.

A native *'olapalapa* tree stretches its slender branches across the cave entrance, shivering as its leaves catch the light breezes. The rare tree, growing only at high altitudes in Hawaiian swamps, has white wood that burns when it's green. Hula girls in the old days were called *'olapa* because they wiggled so much.

The tree offers a good perch for island birds, and curious over the rare visit of humans, they flock there. Birds seen nowhere else in the world are silhouetted against the overcast sky, perched on the mossy branches, singing unfamiliar calls and seemingly oblivious to the rain pouring from everything.

Once I got lost on a photographic mission to Wai'ale'ale with Dick Davis, who was carrying most of my camera gear. We had been chopping our way through the featureless jungle, finding no sign of the summit trail, when Dick suddenly stopped swinging his machete, and called me to look. Straight ahead of us was the fresh path we had cut not an hour ago. We had tramped in a circle and were lost.

Our predicament was serious, and we immediately climbed a tree to see what there was to see. The sky was overcast and misty. Every tree was the same height and all we looked into were the upper branches of more trees. The old Boy Scout trick of finding north from the side of the tree growing moss didn't work here. Moss several inches thick grew all around the slender branches I held onto, and when I squeezed a new branch, it squirted like a clam.

We held still, watching the sensitive *'olapalapa* respond to the slight breezes, and after a half hour we agreed on the direction the wind was blowing. We stared at the rain clouds for minutes at a time, turning our heads to what we thought was the brightest spot in the darkness. We didn't notice any birds on the ground, but as we waited silently in the tree they flew over to look at us, perching within arms' reach on the wet branches.

Acting upon a unanimous vote, we decided the direction we should go and set out again. We had a map, but no compass, and the map was virtually worthless because we were not quite sure where we had started out from. Eventually we stumbled upon a stream we had encountered on our way in, and we retraced our steps back to camp. We returned considerably more aware of the danger of overconfidence in the Kaua'i wilderness.

Robert Wenkam is a photographer and author of six Hawai'i books, including *Kaua'i and the Park Country of Hawai'i*. He lives in Honolulu.

Saying Aloha

....

A Pilialoha with Pele

Searching for Aiko

Sherry Lee

The Last Aloha

August Butterflies

Madame Pele speaks in curious ways—with great dramatic bursts of fire and smoke, and with subtle clues that often can be read only by a certain few. In this Hawai'i memoir, Michael Sturrock recalls a display that signified . . .

A Pilialoha
with Pele

I was fourteen years old the year Kīlauea Iki erupted, and it was, truly, unforgettable. The volcano began erupting in November 1959 and it continued erupting quite a while. Through the months that followed the beginning of the eruption, the sky over the Hawaiian Islands got very red because of all the ash in the atmosphere.

If I remember correctly, the eruption had a fire spume two thousand feet high, and the ash that accumulated in the atmosphere over the Islands created brilliant sunsets.

One evening while I was reading the *Honolulu Star Bulletin*, I looked at a picture on page one that showed the extent of the ash cloud over the entire Hawaiian Islands, and, you know, it looked oddly familiar.

I just started turning the newspaper around until there it was—the cloud formation was in the shape of the Big Island of Hawai'i, where the eruption was occurring.

When I saw this, I commented to my mother that Pele must be putting on this fire show in honor of her old friend Uncle George Lycurgus, who had died at 101 years of age during the eruption.

For most of the second half of his life, Uncle George—that's what everyone called him—had watched over the Volcano House at Kīlauea and had developed a *pilialoha*, or close companionship, with Pele.

To this day, as I look back on this event, I feel it was Pele's way of saying aloha to her old friend.

Dr. Michael Kekahimoku Sturrock, a native of Hawai'i and a Kamehameha Schools graduate, lives in Bellevue, Washington, where he is a veterinarian. His family originates from Kohala on the island of Hawai'i, where he spent his boyhood summers in Waimea and learned to appreciate the power of Pele.

Looking for ancestors in Hawai'i can lead to strange places, like a long-neglected, almost forgotten graveyard in Hilo. Sometimes, the result is a great surprise, as a Maui woman discovers when she goes . . .

Searching for Aiko

A Chinese man from Canton named Aiko has been part of our family lore for as far back as I can remember. I was fascinated by this ancestor, partly because when I looked in the mirror at my round, brown eyes and freckled nose, there was no hint of this connection.

Aiko was even more of a mystery because he arrived, alone, in Honolulu on a sailing ship engaged in the China Trade somewhere in the early 1800s—years before Chinese laborers were imported to work the sugarcane fields of Hawai'i.

Unlike the other Chinese who trickled into the islands in those early days, he showed no compulsion to return to his homeland. Was he running from a past of violence and poverty? Had he no family, no beliefs that pulled him back as did the other Chinese?

One thing we know about Aiko was that he was industrious. Before long he was managing lands in the Kohala district of the Big Island for Kamehameha III, and had set up a small sugar mill and begun producing a crude brown whiskey product in the tradition of China.

We know he was reasonable, and kind—even democratic for his time. He married a Hawaiian woman from the district, and when her 'ohana complained that he had dammed up their water supply for the production of his sugar, he stopped immediately and apologized.

Later, when the family closed the Kohala mill and moved to the then-prosperous town of Hilo, he resumed sugar planting, bought a movie theater and pool hall, and adopted the Chinese-Hawaiian son of another Chinese who had returned to China. He even converted to Catholicism, and in his will left his money (considerable by this time) to his only daughter, Amelia, with strict instructions that it should be for her alone, and not available to her husband. Something almost revolutionary for the late nineteenth century, and even much more so for an Asian.

Aiko lived well into his nineties, although by the end he was nearly blind. My grandmother remembers him sitting on their porch along Waiānuenue Avenue smoking a pipe and listening to the children play in the yard. When he died, he was buried in St. Joseph's Catholic Cemetery nearby, on land he had given to the church.

I was recently in Hilo on a writing assignment with a few hours to kill before catching my plane, and thought I'd try to find the legendary (at least in our family) Aiko's grave. It seemed like an easy task. Only when I asked, no one knew where St. Joseph's graveyard was. I finally found someone in the church office who thought it must be the old abandoned one a few streets over, tucked behind a parking lot and housing project.

I made my way to the spot, climbing through weeds and a broken fence. The graveyard was one of the oldest in Hilo, and neglected. Headstones were sometimes visible, sometimes not, as I wound my way trying to locate a familiar family name. I found what must have once been our family plot. It was covered with brush, but there were the names of long-forgotten "Victors" (an Anglicized name for the Hawaiian "Wikoli"). But no Aiko.

I searched awhile more, but gave up eventually, and

headed toward the gate to leave. Suddenly in the warm, noonday sun something told me to stop. To try again. "Okay, Aiko," I said to myself. "If you want to be found, you're going to have to show me where you are!"

I turned and walked back to where I had found the other family graves. There was no Aiko, just more bushes. Then in that miraculous way things like this work, I got a hunch, a big hunch. I climbed over graves and began spreading the high brush apart. The branches parted and there he was.

Not more than six feet from me at eye level was a large stone with the name "Aiko" simply chiseled. A warm feeling came over me. It was like a friendly smile from long ago—reaching across the generations, saying "Hello. Here I am. I'm glad I mattered."

Educated at the Kamehameha Schools and the University of Oregon, Kaui Philpotts is a freelance author specializing in food and travel. Winner of the Penney-Missouri Award for Journalism and the 1995 Big Island of Hawai'i Journalism Award in the Arts, Culture, and Food category, she is the author of several books and a contributor to numerous magazines. Her story "The Saltbox House" appeared in *Hawai'i's Best Spooky Tales* (1997).

Sometimes when a person is dying they may urge family members to mend a broken relationship, patch up an old wound. In this poignant story, a Kaua'i man receives a message from his terminally ill niece in a dream, and heeds the last wishes of . . .

Sherry Lee

Family feuds happen in the best of families, and my family is no exception.

My brother Paul and I once had one of the closest brother-brother relationships that anyone could want. But in the late 1970s, we parted and went separate ways.

Paul was a career Army man, who traveled to Germany, Korea, Okinawa, and Stateside. He had a daughter named Sherry Lee, who was well aware of the relationship her father and I had. During Paul's tour in Aberdeen, Maryland, Sherry Lee was diagnosed with leukemia. I was not aware of Sherry Lee's medical condition, since I was not corresponding with Paul.

Paul was reassigned to Hawai'i and stationed at Fort Shafter. During that time, Sherry Lee was receiving chemotherapy at Tripler Army Medical Center.

On the morning of September 20, 1979, between 2:00 a.m. and 4:00 a.m., I did not know if I was awake or if I was dreaming, but I saw Sherry Lee descending from the sky, dressed in white. She looked like an angel, but she did not have any wings. She came closer and closer, and then stood next to my bedside and told me to "Please talk to my father. He really misses you, but does not know how to go about communicating with you again."

I said okay, I will try, and then Sherry Lee disappeared.

Later that morning, I called my family in Honolulu, to

find out that Sherry Lee was at Tripler Army Medical Center and was not doing too well. I then called my mother and asked her if she wanted to go to Honolulu and see Sherry Lee the next day.

On September 21, 1979, my mom and I went to Honolulu and went straight to the hospital. To my shock and amazement, Sherry Lee was on a life support unit, bald, and lying almost lifeless on the bed. I could not believe the condition she was in. She was not like how I saw her in my dream.

Other family members were present, and someone said, "Let's all go to the other room and pray for Sherry Lee." Dumbfounded, I followed the rest of the family, and we held hands and formed a circle and prayed for her.

My nephew started praying for Sherry Lee's release from the pain that she was suffering. I was again in more shock. I did not expect to pray for Sherry Lee's release, but to pray for her to get better.

After the prayer, we went to see Sherry Lee in the other room. I watched in a trance as the lines on the monitor above her bed went from wavy lines to just a straight line—and then just a plain beep. Sherry Lee had died.

A nurse came in and disconnected all the wires and tubes from Sherry Lee's body and then covered her face with the sheet. The nurse expressed her sympathy and then left us standing there in awe. On September 26, five days later, Sherry Lee was laid to rest at Punchbowl Cemetery, the National Cemetery of the Pacific, under a little tree.

I recently visited Sherry Lee's gravesite and noticed that the little tree has grown and that it now shades her resting place. Last September was the twentieth anniversary of her death. May her soul rest in peace.

My brother Paul and I are at peace also.

Richard S. Fukushima was born and raised on Kauaʻi. He attended the University of Hawaiʻi and Kauaʻi Community College and served in the United States Army and the Hawaiʻi Army National Guard. He currently works at the Hanapēpē Public Library. A widower, he enjoys golf, bowling, fishing, cooking, quilting, and writing poetry and short articles. His story "Mamoru" appeared in *Hawaiʻi's Best Spooky Tales: True Local Spine-Tinglers*, and his story "The *Holoholo* Man" appeared in *Hawaiʻi's Best Spooky Tales 2*.

The last day in Hawai'i is difficult, especially for anyone who's lived in the Islands. The last day is like the last day of a life in the sun. Some spend their last day at the beach, or in the warm embrace of the sea.

On her last day in Hawai'i, a lone woman snorkeler finds herself suddenly in the company of scary creatures who may have come to bid . . .

The Last Aloha

It was my last day in Hawai'i before we moved back to Tulsa. My husband and I spent that last day in the ocean snorkeling the reef at Lanikai, one of our favorite weekend pastimes. We were always in the water in those days.

He liked to go way out beyond the Mokulua Islands on his kayak and then dive. I liked to stay closer in, near the reef, where I saw, all in the space of a minute on that last day, things I'd never seen on that otherwise benign reef before, things that scared the devil out of me! Talk about chicken skin!

The first thing I saw was a very large fish, much larger then I'd ever seen there. I just came around the reef and there it was about four feet away. It startled me, and as I turned around, there was a *honu kai* five feet away. I'd never seen one that close to shore before, nor ever while snorkeling in that area.

I jumped out of the water, and steadied myself on the reef. As I glanced down to check my hand on the reef, there was a moray eel waving in the current a foot away from not just my hand, but my whole body!

That did it! I turned to get out of there, and saw swimming toward me fast, definitely targeting me, a menacing looking fin. I nearly had a heart attack before I realized it was only my husband, Faust, who had been gone for two hours, snorkeling further out, whom I didn't expect to see the rest of the afternoon!

Now when I remember that day I like to think the creatures of the reef were coming to say *aloha*.

Suzan Gray Bianco is a jazz singer, a grandmother, and a former resident of Lanikai. She and her husband, Faust, a clinical psychologist, live in Oklahoma now, but return often to Hawai'i on frequent snorkeling and kayaking trips.

Often in Hawai'i, I have been alone in distant places—a boat far out to sea, a summit of an island, or a quiet place near home. Suddenly, a single, fluttering butterfly appears. I always wonder: What is a butterfly doing here? I should have wondered: What if the butterfly is not a butterfly at all? An ancient Chinese and Japanese belief, some say superstition, is that souls of the dead can, and often do, return to visit the living in the form of a butterfly—often a white cabbage butterfly. In Hawai'i, today, butterflies often make surprise appearances, as you will discover in this poignant trilogy by three eyewitnesses.

August Butterflies

In August 1991 my favorite dog died. She was ill, and so we had her put to sleep. She was very much a part of me—knew when I was down, would stare at me until I woke up if I overslept—you know, that kind of dog.

Coincidentally, the next day I had to fly from Honolulu to Hilo, since my grandmother was ill. She passed away the day I arrived. Aunty said she had been waiting for me to get there.

To this day I can't remember the exact date. It was in August, but for some reason I have blanked out when exactly.

In August 1998, my cousin, who recently graduated from the University of California at Irvine, was visiting his sister on O'ahu. He was returning to California after visiting his folks in Hilo.

Early one morning, he and his sister and I went for a hike up Diamond Head. We were remembering Grandma and talking about her as we returned to my house together.

In my yard we were greeted by three butterflies. One for each of us. One was just emerging—all wet and fresh and new and resting.

My mom came out of the house then and reminded us: it was the seventh anniversary of Grandma's death.

Claire Ikehara is a librarian at the Salt Lake/Moanalua Public Library.

NYLA FUJII-BABB

In October of 1992 my first husband, Warren, died after a long and painful struggle with cancer. We had been happily married for twenty-three years. I took care of him at home in the last days of his illness. My daughter and I were the ones who closed his eyes for the last time and said good-bye.

Though he was an only and eldest son, my mother-in-law quietly told me that she hoped I would marry again someday, because she did not want me to be alone. What a special woman! But I did not think remarriage was very likely, since I was well into my forties by then, with a nearly grown-up daughter.

Three years later, during an all-day program I was producing at a shopping center in town, I met a very gentlemanly blues musician named Jeff. He had come to the gig expecting to do some sound engineering for one of the bands I had hired. Seeing that I had no sound engineer for the rest of the day and no money to pay for one, he graciously offered to do the sound for all of our performers. That evening, as we shared a Korean plate lunch dinner, he was able to make me laugh—something I hadn't done for a long time. At the end of dinner, he asked me to come and see his band play later that week and I did!

In August 1995, Jeff and I took a little trip to the Big Island. I had spent my first honeymoon on the Big Island, and my small family of three had vacationed there many times.

It was with some doubt and pain that I returned. It was a sad and a happy time.

On the Hāmākua Coast there is a beach park called

Kolekole Beach Park. Over the years, the river that runs down to the sea there had become one of my family's favorite play spots. When Jeff and I returned in August, I was reluctant to visit the park, but we went down anyway. Jeff kindly allowed me a few minutes alone with my memories.

As he walked down to look at the waves of the beach, I stayed by the river and talked with Warren, asking him if I was doing the right thing and if it would be okay.

When Jeff returned, suddenly there appeared a white butterfly, flying around and around me and then flying around and around both of us.

It stayed for a long while, then flew up into the air and disappeared. I told Warren thank you—and a year later, Jeff and I were married.

Nyla Fujii-Babb has been a professional storyteller, actress, and producer in Hawai'i and on the mainland for over twenty-five years. She is currently the Children's Librarian at the Salt Lake/Moanalua Public Library.

MARY ANN COLLIGNON

It was my first death since childhood days. I wasn't prepared for the loss of my mother, even though I am a middle-aged adult, and my mom was in her seventies.

Growing up, it had just been the two of us for as long as I could remember—a single parent and an only child. As is often the case, two independent "women," parent and child, were frequently at loggerheads.

After my mom died, I fully expected a message or a sign from her.

She had held onto life tenaciously, despite being on a respirator for two weeks following emergency open-heart surgery. During that time, I did all the talking, which must have driven her crazy. Much of the communication on her part was eye contact, slight nods of the head, and in the end, just the posture of basic body language.

"Let's go see your mom," my husband said, the morning after her funeral.

We headed out to the cemetery, the "duck pond," drop-off point for many Easter ducklings over the years, as well as a beautiful tree-filled park and the final resting place for many of the town's human residents.

I mentioned my expectations of a message from Mom and laughingly recounted the previous night at her house when I had passed by the turned-off television and thought I heard voices coming from it. I finally determined that the dispatch being picked up was not at all heavenly, but something more earthbound—like local truckers.

Walking down the hill to Mom's gravesite, we spotted a small yellow butterfly darting in and out of flowers on the grave.

"Well," I said, looking at my husband with a laugh, "that's a little more gentle than I would have expected!"

As we started to leave, a loud crash occurred behind us.

Turning, we just caught sight of a twenty-foot tree limb falling to the ground.

"That's more Mom's style," I said.

On the way home, we stopped to see Mom's best friend.

While we were standing, talking, in her driveway, a large, sturdy brown butterfly landed on my knee. It stayed for so long, someone finally said, "Shoo it away."

But I was intrigued by its licking presence on my knee, and I thought: "Oh, butterfly kisses!"

A few days later, when touching base with a friend and co-worker in Hawai'i, I laughingly said that I had been looking for a message or sign from Mom.

Suddenly, my friend said, "Have you seen a butterfly?"

I said I had, indeed, seen two.

That's when I learned for the first time of the Asian belief that the soul of the departed comes for a final farewell in the form of a butterfly. I remembered the butterfly kisses, and I felt comforted.

A week later, another friend and I were preparing the house for my mom's estate sale. As we were carrying things into the house, another brown butterfly, just like the other one, landed on my shoulder.

"Brush it off so it doesn't get trapped in the house," I said.

My friend did, and then I realized with a start— "Mom!" I ran back outside only to see the butterfly flying out of the yard.

I quickly realized that Mom must have come back one last time to make sure her six much-beloved cats were okay and to say good-bye to them.

One final "butterfly" appeared when among Mom's things I found a quilt that had been started by my grandmother and finished by my mom—a blue sky background covered entirely in butterflies!

Mary Ann Collignon is the Young Adult Librarian at Salt Lake/Moanalua Public Library. Mililani is now home, along with her husband, Larry, "who always has thought I was just a little spooky," and Moose, Max, and Sweet Pea—felines extraordinaire. "We love you, Mom, and miss you! Thanks for the kisses."

Royal Encounters

Lament for a Dead Princess

Queen Emma Returns to the Summer Palace

The Place Where Kalākaua Died

King Kamehameha the Great, born under Halley's Comet, died in 1819. His final resting place, "known only to the moon and the stars," remains one of Hawai'i's great unsolved mysteries. Other mysterious tales, some quite recent, involve Queen Lili'uokalani, Princess Ka'iulani, Queen Emma, and King Kalākaua. Here are three of my favorite .

Royal Encounters

Lament for a Dead Princess

When Queen Lili'uokalani died at age seventy-nine, it was said volcanoes erupted and the seas turned an odd hue due to the large schools of red fish that swarmed in the tides.

Peacocks cried when Princess Ka'iulani died, according to Kristin Zambucka, who wrote a book about the princess's life and death.

Princess Ka'iulani, she said, died at 2:00 a.m. on March 6, 1899, at 'Āinahau, her home in Waikīkī. She called out a single muffled word and died, and the room became still. She was twenty-three.

For miles around, people knew the exact hour of her death, because her pet peacocks began screaming loudly and kept shrieking until sunrise.

A few days before the centennial of her death, I received an e-mail from Hawai'i Nation Info (info@hawaii-nation.org):

"If any of you are still awake at 2:00 tomorrow morning, listen carefully—maybe you can hear the ghost of those peacocks screaming again, exactly 100 years later, in grief for Ka'iulani, the last hope of the Kalākaua dynasty."

That night, I slept without hearing a sound, but now each time I hear a peacock crying in Hawai'i it turns my head and I wonder.

Queen Emma Returns to the Summer Palace

If you've been to Queen Emma's Summer Palace in O'ahu's Nu'uanu Valley, you already know that the queen herself, although dead now for more than a century, sometimes is seen walking about the garden, or sitting on her lanai. So I've been told.

When I visit the summer palace nothing unusual happens, but then I've never been invited to spend the night during a full moon, which apparently is when Queen Emma prefers to revisit her summer palace.

One day, according to Erna Fergusson, the author of *Our Hawaii*, Queen Emma left a souvenir of her nightly visit. Several friends, Fergusson wrote, were invited to spend the night at the summer palace on a full-moon night. A man sleeping alone in a bedroom under the eaves woke up suddenly in the middle of the night to see an old Hawaiian woman enter his room.

He sat up to speak to her, but she approached without saying a word, put her hand on his chest and pushed him back on the bed, where he fell into a deep sleep. He awoke the next morning, thinking it was only a dream.

Before breakfast, he joined other guests at the pool for a swim.

"Oh, so you slept in the little room under the eaves," a man said.

"Why yes, how did you know?"

"The mark on your chest."

He looked down at his chest. There was the faint out-line of a red handprint the size of a woman's hand.

The Palace Where Kalākaua Died

On his way back to Hawai'i from Europe in 1891, King David Kalākaua, the last reigning king of the Hawaiian Islands, suffered a stroke and died, January 20, in a palace in San Francisco—the Sheraton Palace Hotel. He was fifty-four.

In the centennial year of his death, I stayed at the grand old hotel, intending to write an article for *Hawai'i* magazine about His Majesty's last night on Earth.

My request to spend the night in Kalākaua's death room was politely declined. I spent the night in a royal suite with complimentary French champagne, but it was not what I wanted.

It's a mystery to me why nobody would tell me the number of the monarch's death chamber; the hotel keepers don't want people to know a Hawaiian king died in their hotel, I guess. Other important people died at The Palace, and their deaths in no way reflected on the hotel's first-class service and hospitality. People die, sometimes in hotels.

In honor of Hawai'i's last monarch, I think the Sheraton Palace should affix a brass plaque in his memory, create a historic shrine to Kalākaua, complete with tropical flowers. Many Hawaiians I know might want to visit the room or even spend the night. Few people today know he died in San Francisco, and nobody I knew had ever been to the room.

One night at a dinner party at the old Kahala Hilton, several of us talked about strange things that have happened in hotels, here and elsewhere, and I was surprised to hear Mary Lou Foley say she and two other Hawai'i women visited Kalākaua's death site at the Sheraton Palace several years ago and that something strange happened.

A Filipino bellhop, she said, took them to Room 810, and they all held their breath as he unlocked the door and ushered them into the room.

Mary Lou said it was probably just her imagination, but the room was close, and she felt a spiritual presence.

"I can't really explain it," she said. "It was just weird being there knowing that's where Kalākaua died."

When the women looked at the bed, they saw a kind of depression and they got overcome by who knows what—anxiety, grief, or emotion—and had to leave. Mary Lou said it was hard to explain, but something seemed to be present in that room. I asked one of the other three women to recall her impressions of the visit to Kalākaua's death site and she told me a similar story.

I plan to reserve Room 810 next January 20, the anniversary of Kalākaua's death, and spend the night. Of course, I'll let you know what, if anything, happens.

Rick Carroll is the collector and editor of *Hawai'i's Best Spooky Tales*. He also contributed "Rick's Encounters" on page 137.

Personal Encounters

Forbidden Village

On the Beach

When Kūpuna Fly

Old Bones

The Halloween Waiter

When anyone asks what strange encounters I've experienced in Hawai'i I usually say, "Oh nothing really, stuff like that always happens to someone else." It's easier than admitting to uneasy moments on the "forbidden" island of Ni'ihau, or recalling the night a hand appeared in the zoom lens of my camera on a deserted Kaua'i beach, and the day I met a woman on Maui whose father missed his own funeral on Lana'i. Then I decided to take my own advice and write down a few eerie encounters that appear here for the first time in this personal collection of six stories.

Personal Encounters

Forbidden Village

You can go to the forbidden Island of Niʻihau by heli-copter, and I have, twice, but you can't visit the village of Puʻuwai (pop. 180). It's still *kapu*, off-limits, the last Hawaiʻi place to keep its secret.

The first time I landed on Niʻihau, spiraling down clockwise from the present day, I'd hoped to see the vil-lage whose name in Hawaiian means "heart," but the only living creatures in evidence were a wild pig on its last legs and a swarm of white-tipped sharks in an emerald bay. I walked a deserted beach and left without meeting a soul. It didn't seem very aloha-like.

On my second visit I did see the village but only from a great distance.

Two women and two little girls met us on the lava bed on Niʻihau's raw south coast. The older woman carried a handmade Bible; the other brought bananas and neck-laces of tiny red and white and yellow seashells once worn by Hawaiʻi's queens.

Shy at first, they spoke English softly and when they spoke Hawaiian to each other, it sounded like music. I asked what life was like on the island, but they pretended not to understand and offered no answers. We smiled a lot and talked slowly about bananas, the Bible, and seashells.

Out beyond the lava, where sand dunes rose and *kiawe* brush flourished, I thought I saw a man on horseback. Something was moving out there. Whatever it was never revealed itself; it was always just around the edges, in the corner of my eye.

Soon, I felt someone staring at me. The hard looks came from Momi, an island girl of ten, who had never known any other place. She studied my eyes, my nose, my teeth, everything about me, and then, in a flash, announced her finding.

"You are a good man," she said. I laughed at her quick study and profound insight and we became instant pals. I felt a kinship with all the sailors who ever jumped ship in the days of Captain Cook.

In the distance, over her thin shoulder, I noticed a gray haired man in dungarees unloading a skiff on the beach. He looked like a castaway, Robinson Crusoe, and as I raised my camera with zoom lens for a closer look, a hand grabbed my hand.

"Come," Momi said, "let's look for shells."

She towed me down to the water's edge. Soon, she had so many shells they spilled from her hand. I found six. Momi laughed and gave me hers.

I looked around, again, for the gray-haired man in dungarees, but he was gone. The woman with the Bible saw him, too, and said he was Bruce Robinson, the man who owns Niʻihau, the man who inherited Niʻihau from his seafaring New Zealand forebears.

I wondered why he never came over to say hello? Or how are you? I wondered if I had really even seen him, the ghost *luna* of Niʻihau. Except for Momi, I have never felt so unwelcome on any island in the Pacific.

After shelling, Momi and I went snorkeling in a crystal-clear lagoon full of polychromatic fish that reflected our laughter and joy and life itself.

Offshore, not too far from us, the deep blue water boiled, and we sensed a commotion underwater and lifted our masks and stood in the lagoon, open-mouthed, snorkels on our chin, watching whales, the most whales I have ever seen in Hawaiian waters—spy-hopping, chin-slapping whales, tail-slapping, fluking whales, jumping straight out of the water. The dance of the whales—Hawaiians would call it a sign—ended as abruptly as it had begun. We applauded. Momi and I. We didn't know what else to do.

Eager to explore on my own, I took off down the empty beach littered with rusty Spam cans and other Pacific junk and soon found myself out of sight of Momi and the others. I felt uneasy, uncomfortable, as if some primal thing lay in wait behind the dunes. Something was watching me, I knew, to make sure I didn't violate the forbidden island's *kapu* and venture on deeper into the island, seeking entry to Puʻuwai. My secret mission was known, telegraphed before my arrival; I was herded, kept apart from truths.

I saw the man on horseback again, but he was only a dark, disappearing shadow in the *kiawe*. I turned back, glad to rejoin the others. The two women seemed relieved to see me back in their company. Momi and her sister grabbed my hands and did a little girl dance of joy.

When we took off, I thought Momi would wave her arm off as the chopper rose off the black lava. I knew I would never see her again. We buzzed the islet of Lehua, then swung counterclockwise around Niʻihau, returning to our reality.

Tom, our pilot, buzzed empty beaches low enough to kick up sand, we hovered over a wrecked yacht on a coral reef that guarded a gold sand beach, chased wild pigs with our rotor racket and ground shadow, peered at white-tipped sharks chasing their tales in jade lagoons.

Observing the *kapu* of the island, we swung wide and far out to sea, and there it was: the forbidden village. The sun was off to our right, and the glass canopy of the helicopter seemed to magnify, like an insect on a pin, the tiny museum-piece village of Pu'uwai. A coastal cluster of clapboard houses at the end of a sand road through thorn bush. The last Hawaiian place. Hawai'i, past and future.

With naked eye and zoom lens I looked long and hard but saw no people, no sign of life. It was like glimpsing the past, an Old West ghost town-—early *'āina*, post-Contact.

I stared at the forbidden village stuck right there in sand until it grew smaller and vanished from sight. As we flew on, I tried to imagine what life was like down there, but already it was too far in the past. It felt good to keep moving back into the future, to my own life and times.

I don't know why, but I still have the tiny shells Momi found that day.

On the Beach

Wind was howling at 30 knots, and the pounding waves were big as houses as we walked on the beach on Kaua'i's North Shore just before sunset. We were the only ones on the beach, and I wanted to go but Marcie didn't; she was beachcombing, lost in her own world on this empty, storm-swept October beach.

I know it was October, because we always spent October in Hanalei in those days, kicking back, reading in the sun, trying to decide which beach to have all to ourselves.

We spent days bobbing in the surf counting waterfalls, and most nights hanging out at Tahiti Nui with Auntie Louise, Frenchy and Larry, and Christian and the gang. It was all ukuleles, lime-laced rum drinks, and endless refrains of "Hanalei Moon" back then.

That October day, a storm blew in from the North Pacific and we set out to search for glass balls, those floats that disentangle from Japanese fishing nets and wash ashore like gems.

The big surf made me uneasy, but I knew Marcie wouldn't leave until she found a treasure. I turned my back on the waves and lifted my camera to take her picture, and that's when I saw a single hand rising up behind her from the sand at the base of the cliff.

I signaled to her to come toward me and she did. I looked back once and saw the hand waving, but couldn't tell if it was beckoning or shooing us away. It could have been a couple making love on the beach. Or a trap. We were from San Francisco then, not *akamai* to island ways. Instead of investigating further, we left the beach slowly.

I did stop at Waininha Store to use the rusty pay phone to report a suspicious situation to Hanalei Police. As we drove back to our cottage, we could hear sirens screaming around the mile-long crescent of Hanalei Bay, slowing for each single-lane bridge, until they fell silent at the beach and men ran across hard sand to rescue the fallen soul.

A few days later, I read in the *Garden Island News* that a volunteer fireman named Danny, while searching for surfers presumed lost in high surf, slipped off the crumbly cliff by the highway with no guard rail and fell to the beach, breaking his back.

The paper further said that a San Francisco beach-comber (and "part-time resident of Hanalei") spotted Danny on the beach by chance in his camera's zoom lens. It said Danny would have been scoured out to sea by the big waves in the next high tide if I hadn't seen him. I was surprised to see my name in print, and for a moment I felt like some kind of hero, but then wished I'd gone immediately to his aid instead of only alerting authorities.

One day, a year or two later, I stopped by Tahiti Nui to see my old friend Christian Marston. It was in-between lunch and dinner, and no one was in the restaurant, so I went back to the kitchen to see if he was there. As I walked in, a young and beautiful Hawaiian woman suddenly grabbed me and gave me a big kiss. It was Haunani Ah Sing, the wife of my friend Christian, with something else in common.

"Mahalo for saving my friend Danny," she said.

When Kūpuna Fly

From the air, Kaua'i is one of the most beautiful islands in the Pacific. In my book, it ranks right up there with Bora Bora and Huahine. Each time I fly over Kaua'i I think how wonderful it would be if everyone who lives there could see their island from on high—the impenetrable Nā Pali Coast, ever-changing Waimea Canyon, and Wai'ale'ale crater, which looks like a lost kingdom in the clouds.

One day I met Ku'ulei Mahina, who works at 'Ohana Helicopters, the only one on Kaua'i, owned and operated by Bogart Kealoha, an ex–Honolulu Fire Department rescue chopper pilot. Mahina told me they had started taking native Kauaians fifty-five and older on free helicopter rides over their island.

Something to look forward to, if you live Kaua'i.

"It's the owner's way of saying thank you for putting up with us," Mahina said. "A way of returning the island back to the people of the island."

Whenever they have an empty seat, they put a *kupuna* in the chopper with tourists and off they go. It's a learning experience for everyone, she said.

"We've flown, all told, about twenty *kūpuna* so far," she said. "They cry up there, it's real spiritual and uplifting for them to see their island from the air. The majority of the *kūpuna* have never flown in a helicopter before. A lot of them get chicken skin.

"We flew one *kupuna* twice," she said, "Elethia Okuna of Omao, Kaua'i, in her late sixties. We adopted her, she's like family. It meant a lot to her to go a second time because her son's ashes were scattered over Wai'ale'ale. She threw a handful of flowers in the crater and said aloha."

Old Bones

We sat at Orchids at Halekūlani one golden Waikīkī after-noon, talking about old Hawaiian bones that surfaced in sand dunes of Kapalua, Maui, when the Ritz-Carlton Hotel was built nearly a decade ago.

It was an odd encounter—two militant Hawaiian men, Clifford Naeole and Lopaka, and the public relations woman for the Ritz Carlton. It was her idea to get us together.

"Every day more and more bones surfaced," Lopaka said. "It got to the point where it was too much. Enough was enough."

"How many burials?" I asked.

"About twelve hundred," he said. "Nobody knew it was that extensive. They just had a few when they started taking them out."

The unearthing of ancestral Hawaiian bones happened in 1990, but Lopaka was still angry, a sullen Hawaiian not yet at peace.

"All over the state," he said, "it's been done, but this time we protested, we stopped the construction, we forced the hotel to move away from the graveyard.

"Personally, I did the reburial work," Lopaka said. "It was spiritual, real spooky, handling the bones of my ances-tors."

We shivered a little in the tropical sun.

"It was hard for me to go to the hotel, even be there," he said. "They were bad people, they didn't move out of the kindness of their heart; they were forced to, I mean it was like they fought it all they way, they were forced, but they had no choice. If they had their way, they would have put the hotel on the coast."

The public relations woman for the Ritz-Carlton Hotel at Kapalua looked nervous but I noticed tears in her eyes. "Don't you think anyone was sensitive to the issue?"

"Well, personally, no," Lopaka said, and Clifford Naeole agreed.

Everyone laughed nervously.

"It was an outrageous act, but something good came out in the end, though," Naeole said.

"It was really hard to deal with the hotel," Clifford said. I would never want to go there, never want to be associated with them until I saw some of the programs that they sponsored, and I felt they really care about the place.

"You know," he said, "it took a while, but finally I decided these people are good people and should be forgiven."

The public relations woman for the Ritz Carlton Hotel gave a faint smile that flashed bright as the glare off the waves at Waikīkī. The sensitive moment had been met and then some.

Today, the sand dune area at Kapalua, where twelve hundred Hawaiian bones were unearthed, is now held in perpetual trust. There are signs that say, Kapu, no trespassing, where the hotel originally was to be built. Often, I have seen tourists pay no heed to the *kapu* signs; they walk across the old Hawaiian graveyard as if it were a golf course.

Strange things, restless things, sometimes happen at The Ritz-Carlton Hotel, and I have experienced them. Doors open and close, there are shadows in the halls on certain moonlit nights, and sometimes the elevators seem to have a mind all their own. It's enough to make you wonder if everyone, living or dead, is at peace.

The Halloween Waiter

I sat down to dinner one Halloween evening at The Lodge at Kō‘ele, and the waiter appeared at my elbow. He looked so stiff and un-Hawaiian in his white dinner jacket, holding a burgundy leather menu.

"Good evening," he said—not aloha, but good evening in proper English.

"Hello," I replied, and smiled.

He handed me the menu and wine list.

"I can't tarry," I said. "I'm reading from my books after dinner."

"I know you are," the waiter said. "I've got a spooky story to tell you."

"I'd like to hear it."

"Certainly, sir."

It was the perfect place to be on Halloween, since The Lodge at Kō‘ele was built on or very near an old grave-yard.

The Halloween waiter began to tell me how when the Lodge first opened, an advertising agency hired a beauti-ful young woman and a handsome young fellow to pose as rich honeymooners.

"They stood outside their suite on the second floor and looked down into The Great Lobby," the waiter said. "They took lots of pictures.

"When the brochure came out, there was the young couple, but standing behind them were other people. Faint outlines of other people. Not shadows, other peo-ple. They threw away the brochures. Tossed 'em. Junk. Took new pictures."

"I'd like to see a copy of the original brochure," I told him.

"I have one at home," he said. "I'll bring it tomorrow."

Next day, the waiter called my room to say he'd looked everywhere and couldn't find the brochure, but that he would keep looking and he would call me when he found it. But I never heard from him again.

I told the young Filipino woman at the Concierge Desk the story I'd heard at dinner and she just hugged her arms, looked around to see who was listening, then said almost in a whisper. "There are many ghosts here."

I called Lānaʻi the other day to ask the Halloween waiter if he ever did find that brochure but when I asked for him by name, I was told that nobody by that name ever worked at The Lodge.